THURNANGL

You are a true hero!
♡ Kimberly Byrd

THURNANGL

KIMBERLY BYRD

iUniverse

THURNANGL

iUniverse books may be ordered through booksellers or by contacting:

iUniverse
1663 Liberty Drive
Bloomington, IN 47403
www.iuniverse.com
1-800-Authors (1-800-288-4677)

ISBN: 978-1-4917-8354-2 (sc)
ISBN: 978-1-4917-8355-9 (e)

Print information available on the last page.

iUniverse rev. date: 12/08/2015

CONTENTS

This book is dedicated to my mother, for all she
has done for me. I love you mom, always.

CHAPTER 1

A PROPHECY

Thurnangl is a land unlike any other, a land where wizards and witches reside. It is filled with a vast array of creatures, many as yet unknown by the people who live there. One might be surprised at the wonders Thurnangl hides.

In the villages, the streets bustle with people. There are the wide open fields of the Northwest that seem to stretch on forever, and to the east and northward are dense mountains covered in thick forest. The trees tower over one's head and hide the sun, shadowing the forest floor. In the South lies the Forest of Mangü, which stretches much further than travelers dare venture. To the far West is the Sea of Ozu, a sea which has swallowed many ships in its dark, treacherous waters. North of The Forest of Mangü is the Swamp of Odswell where the deadliest creatures dwell. In the northernmost reaches of Thurnangl sits the dark land of Garzula with its black mountains which hide dark secrets.

Long ago, this land was cured of a dark sickness by the most powerful wizard. Ozu sacrificed his life, healing Thurnangl to keep the wizards and witches safe. He banded together a small group to restore the land's former wonder and provide refuge from the human world of burning stakes and hangings.

Through his sacrifice to the land, Ozu created the Stone of Power. Its energy and light reflected the very essence of his devotion to his people. The Stone of Power gave unique abilities to certain witches and wizards. Some enabled the gifted one to speak with animals or control plants. Others might grant the ability to heal or to have incredible blacksmithing skills. The list of abilities granted to wizards and witches grew exponentially.

To keep the Stone of Power safe, a select group of wizards and witches used their powerful magic to bury it deep within the ground. The only people in Thurnangl who knew of its location were those who descended directly from those charged with keeping it safe. As the years passed, the wizards and witches with lesser abilities grew envious. They despised those gifted with abilities which they could not possess. They felt overlooked and alienated by the very stone that was meant to bring them together. It was soon decided that they would take fate into their own hands. The angry and envious left Thurnangl and settled in Garzula where they built an army. Thus, a civil war began.

Many people followed and fled to Garzula. Those who stayed in Thurnangl held great power and had no fear of the opposing army. Soon, however, the army of Garzula swelled to outrageous numbers, and its leaders grew ever more powerful. Sürnam, newest and most feared leader of the army, was determined to find the Stone of Power and destroy it, but no one in Garzula knew of its exact location.

In a desperate attempt to find the Stone of Power, Sürnam tore through Thurnangl's lands. He ruthlessly burnt down cities, destroying lives as though trampling blades of grass. With Sürnam as their leader, the army of Garzula grew victorious, and death spread through Thurnangl.

Over the passing years, the people of Thurnangl began to lose hope, until one day, a young wizard came upon a library spreading for miles underground with vast shelves full of ancient spells and incantations. He walked through the library, amazed at its size and gazing in wonder at the power that lay before him.

The young man discovered an enormous scroll on a wall and, upon deciphering it, found it was a Prophecy. The Prophecy spoke of an enormously powerful person with flaming red hair, who would travel to a far off land and bring back the two heroes who would end the war.

The chosen traveler would bring back a girl named Crystal, with shining blonde hair and stunning blue eyes. She would control the elements of air and water, and she would possess the ability to heal. The chosen one would also find a boy named Brant, who would control earth and fire. Brant would prove an astounding swordsman. Together, they would control the four elements.

The young man searched the library, gathering all of the spells and incantations the Prophecy barer would need to accomplish his task. Wasting no time, he immediately traveled to Keldom, the capital city of Thurnangl, and told of the Prophecy. The people searched for months to find the person who fit the Prophecy's description. They found Malchior and shared the Prophecy's secrets with him. Malchior, willing to help his people at any cost, agreed to carry out its great purpose. Before the year was out, Malchior bid goodbye to his pregnant wife and set off after the Stone of Power. Being of such high ranks, as well as the carrier of the Prophecy, he was one of the very few who knew where Stone of Power lay hidden.

As Malchior made his way to the Stone of Power, he was set upon by Sürnam's spies. The evil Sürnam had heard of the Prophecy and was determined to stop it. With the utterance of a single death spell, Malchior was slain, and the Prophecy remained unfulfilled.

Not long after his death, Malchior's wife, Mardra, gave birth to a baby girl and named her Frinz. From her birth, Frinz was special and bore the very same flaming red hair as her father. Mardra knew Frinz was the true carrier of the Prophecy. Mardra kept Frinz a secret from most people in Thurnangl for fear of seeing her child's death. Mardra and the leaders of Thurnangl did all they could to prepare the child for the fate that awaited her. Eighteen years passed before Frinz traveled to the Stone of Power. Drawing the very essence of magic from the stone, she recited the incantation and disappeared in a flash of light.

And so, our story begins.

CHAPTER 2
BRANT & CRYSTAL

Out of all of the people in the world, there were no two closer than Crystal and Brant. They were born on the same day at the very same time, and after spending sixteen years together, they were inseparable. Their families lived close in the woods, not far from their high school.

Crystal was a fun, lighthearted girl who turned serious when needed. Her personality sparkled with joy, and her heart gave love to all. Brant was the type who would defend his friends and family no matter the cost. He was never afraid to show his courage and strength, especially when standing up for others. He was very laid back and tried his best not to let life trouble him, but sometimes it did. Most of the time, those troubles involved Crystal.

As they did every day after school, Brant and Crystal walked home, wrapped in their fall clothing and listening to their feet crunch down the path. They breathed in the crisp fall air and discussed the day's events.

"I bet you anything I failed Mrs. Smith's science test," Crystal said gloomily.

"Oh come on. It wasn't that bad. I think I did pretty well," Brant said with pride.

Crystal gave a heavy sigh and replied, "I'm just glad that it's Friday. This week dragged on forever!"

"Yeah me too," Brant said, smiling up at the trees.

They came to the fork in the road and said their goodbyes, each turning down a different path home. As Crystal walked down the path, leaves fell around her in a beautiful scene. Crystal saw a bright red leaf on the ground and picked it up, thinking of her mother waiting at home. Fall was her mother's favorite season. Crystal smiled. Every moment of fall brought sweet memories of her mother's love.

A ball of light flashed suddenly in front of Crystal's eyes. She turned to follow the light and saw before her a young woman cloaked in a long, blue robe. Crystal could see hair as red as fire under the cloak which shadowed the figure's face. Crystal blinked, and the figure vanished. She shrugged, thinking it nothing more than her imagination, and continued on her way home. When she reached the house, Crystal noticed that the car was not in the driveway. She went inside and took off her jacket, setting her backpack next to the door. Crystal went into the kitchen for a snack and noticed a note from her mother on the counter.

Dear Crystal,

> *Your father and I went out to have dinner with Brant's parents. We'll be back soon.* <u>*Do your homework*</u>

Love, Mom

"Well at least I don't have any homework," Crystal said aloud.

The house was quiet, as it had been since her brother left for college a few months before. Her sister had been away at school for two years, but the new silence since her brother's departure was still noticeable. Brant was an only child and had often told Crystal how much he envied her for having two very close siblings. He was sometimes lonely, and his house was always quiet.

At an early age, Crystal had found the solution. She had constantly encouraged him saying "Well, we'll be really close friends and play all the time. Then you'll never be lonely."

Crystal smiled fondly at the memory.

Taking advantage of the quiet house and eager to read the new book she had borrowed from school, Crystal rushed to her room. She lay down on her bed with her book in front of her, fiddling with the prized gold locket hanging from her neck. She tried to read, but her mind was elsewhere. The image of the cloaked figure returned, haunting her.

As far back as Crystal could remember, her dreams at night swept her away to a magical land. Her dreams revealed a land of magic and wonder, a land where Crystal longed to be. Though her dreams were often foggy, she saw the people and their homes. Sometimes she saw war, which brought fear to her heart. She fought to understand the muddled mess that was her dream, but the details were often hard to understand. She knew the land to be called Thurnangl. She had never told anyone, not even Brant, of the strange dreams she had experienced all of her life. She had always thought people would think her crazy. She disliked not telling her dreams to Brant but knew it would only trouble him. Crystal had not dreamt of Thurnangl for some time, which made the vision on the path much more concerning. Crystal knew the hooded figure well and had followed her through many a dream.

Crystal heard a sudden noise. Cautiously, she put down her book and crept to the stairs. She peered over the stairwell, her heart pounding in her chest. No one was there, and all was silent.

"I guess it was just my imagination," Crystal said as she went back to her room.

Again, she sat on her bed and read a few pages of her book, quiet and calm. A few minutes later, the noise came again. Realizing that there might indeed be an intruder in her home, Crystal grabbed her bedside lamp and rushed downstairs prepared to fight. When Crystal walked through the kitchen and into the living room, she was surprised to see the same hooded woman standing in front of the fireplace, looking at photos of Crystal's family. Crystal froze, and her mind went blank.

The woman looked up at Crystal with a kind smile and said, "It is alright; there is no need to fear me. This is a beautiful picture. You and your family seem to be very happy. Such happy times and memories are hard to capture in Thurnangl."

Crystal blinked. "T-Thurnangl?" she asked, setting the lamp on the floor.

The woman gave a kind smile. "Yes. You see, my name is Frinz, and I came from Thurnangl to find the chosen heroes who would help my people end the civil war that rages in our land. I assume you are Crystal."

"There's no way this is real. I must be hallucinating, or I'm dreaming, or going insane." Crystal closed her eyes, rubbing her temples as she tried to sort everything out in her head. *There is no way something like this could be true. This only happens in books and stories… right?* Crystal asked herself.

Frinz laughed as she casually walked to the couch and sat down. "Fear not. Your mind is in perfect condition, I assure you. I am as real as the sun that rises and sets."

Crystal pondered for a moment, mulling over the woman's words. Finally, with a deep breath, she sat down on the couch next to Frinz. A long moment of silence elapsed as Crystal accepted Frinz's words. Now that Crystal was closer to Frinz, she saw how very beautiful the strange woman was. Frinz's hair was long and curly with locks of flaming red, as though fire itself grew from her head. Her eyes were pools of deep purple, full of kindness and warmth. The clothes she wore were something from ancient stories. A long, green skirt shimmered about her and was accentuated by a simply-woven bodice clinging tightly to her waist.

"If this is real, then the dreams I have had all my life aren't just dreams, right? They must be true, because I saw you in many of them."

Frinz's eyes widened in surprise. "Well I suppose so if you saw me in them. Perhaps it is your specific energy intertwined with the land itself. The Prophecy does not speak of power... Nor are Crystal and Brant even—"

Crystal quickly cut Frinz off. "Wait! Not Brant. Not my best friend since forever, Brant, right? What is he supposed to look like?"

"Brant bears hair of chestnut and eyes of emerald that hold the kindness and wisdom of worlds. He is said to be a protector and kind to all."

Crystal smiled and nodded. "That's Brant. I would know his description anywhere."

"It must be the bond," Frinz whispered to herself.

Crystal blinked and looked at Frinz in confusion. "What did you say?"

Frinz smiled kindly. "Nothing, Crystal. Far too many thoughts for me to comprehend, right now. There is no need to worry."

There was another long lapse of silence between them. Crystal fiddled with her locket nervously.

Crystal thought of Brant and how she had kept her dreams, or visions rather, a secret from him when he was the very one who shared in them. With sudden determination to make things right, Crystal took a deep breath and rose from the couch.

"Where are you going?" Frinz asked, concern etched across her face.

Crystal walked to the door and put on her jacket. "I'm taking you to Brant's house to see if we can get everything between the three of us settled before we do anything else."

Crystal led Frinz outside and down the path to Brant's house. They both kept silent, deep in thought. Crystal's mind was flooded with the guilt of keeping such a secret from her best friend, a secret that affected them together. Her heart gave a pained leap as she wondered what he would think. Frinz was engrossed in thoughts of explaining everything in such a short time. Her charges were so young and from an entirely different world, an entirely different way of life. In their deep thought, neither noticed that they had reached Brant's house. The walk had taken a few short minutes; not nearly enough time for either of them to prepare for what must be said.

Brant was sitting on his bed reading when the doorbell rang. He came downstairs and saw Crystal with the strange young woman standing at her side.

Cautiously he opened the door and asked, "Hey Crystal, who's the guest?"

"Her name is Frinz, and she said she came from Thurnangl," Crystal said, her eyes nervously shifting from Brant to Frinz, who bowed at her introduction.

Brant blinked a few times, as if trying to comprehend what she was telling him. "Frinz from Thurnangl?" He asked as they came inside.

"Yes. That is right, Brant," Frinz said. Her eyes sparkled that the sight of the heroes of the Prophecy, finally together in front of her.

"I guess we have a lot to talk about, huh?" Crystal added guiltily, her cheeks slightly flushed from embarrassment.

Brant let them in, and they sat down on the couch in the living room.

He studied the strange woman's face intently. "As odd as it sounds, I feel like I know you. From dreams...I've had these dreams of a land called Thurnangl. There were—"

"I know," Crystal blurted out. "I've... had them too." She glanced up to see his reaction, only to find him staring back, his gaze a mixture of relief and puzzlement.

Crystal gave a small sigh, relieved yet overwhelmed by the new information before them.

A long silence fell between them. Brant and Crystal glanced fleetingly at one another, but neither knew what to say.

Frinz took a deep breath. "Let me first explain that there is a civil war among my people that has been raging for the last 320 years. Sörnam leads the opposing army with a black heart and an iron fist. His army resides in the dark, dreaded mountains of Garzula. Both sides of this war have had many leaders and followers, but it seems that our numbers, Thurnangl's numbers, have dwindled, and our people are losing hope.

I am here because of a Prophecy thought to be carried out by my father; until he was murdered, and I was born to complete his mission. Many years ago, a young man stumbled upon the Ancient Library. Not many people know where it is, for it holds spells that, when placed in the wrong hands, could be used for dark purposes. In the Ancient Library lies the Prophecy. It foretold that I was to come to your land and take you to Thurnangl to stop this dreaded civil war."

"Um," Crystal interjected, "not to sound rude, but how are we supposed to stop such a war? Brant and I are just two sixteen-year-olds who fail science tests and can't spell!"

"Hey, I'm just fine in Science!" Brant objected.

"Ah, but can you spell?" Crystal retorted with a devilish grin.

Brant fell silent.

Frinz replied sheepishly, "I forgot to mention that you both possess special abilities." As Frinz paused, Crystal and Brant exchanged looks of disbelief. "Crystal, you have the ability to control water and air, and it is said that you have healing abilities. Brant, you carry the power to control earth and fire. You are also an incredible swordsman. Together, you control the four elements. I will lead you through Thurnangl, and we will find your abilities and fulfill the Prophecy. Now, we must go."

"But," Crystal protested, "how can we just leave? What about our parents? And how long will we be in Thurnangl? And don't we need our things?"

"Yeah, we can't just leave! And what if we don't believe you?!" Brant objected loudly, jumping to his feet. He looked into Frinz's eyes intently, trying to find lies in her gaze. He must keep Crystal safe.

Frinz smiled and reassured them. "There is a spell, known only to me, that allows me to stop time between worlds. While you travel with me, time shall not move in your world. As for the time you both shall spend in Thurnangl, that dependent upon when this war ends. And worry not! You will not need your belongings where we are going." Frinz stood, chanting words foreign to Crystal and Brant's ears.

Everything around them froze. A fly that happened to be zooming across the room stopped and was silent. There was no sound—no wind, no leaves rustling. Just silence. Everything was frozen in time.

Crystal looked at Brant, and Brant returned her gaze. There was no longer any doubt. This was real.

Frinz continued, "Here and now, I forewarn you: This task should not be taken lightly. The path you are about to take shall, from this day on, be a long and treacherous one. Hearing the words I have spoken, do you both agree to face what lies ahead?"

Crystal and Brant looked at each other and nodded. Frinz took a deep breath and completed the incantation. "Namashika Moroz Enforn."

Their surroundings swirled in a whirlpool of color. Everything twisted and changed as if it were blending together. When their surroundings ceased moving, Crystal and Brant looked out into the vast land of Thurnangl. A lush, green field spread for miles around them, the grass swaying in the warm breeze of spring air.

CHAPTER 3

ANCIENT SECRETS

Crystal's eyes sparkled with excitement as she studied the landscape around her.

"It's spring!" she exclaimed joyfully.

The field that stretched as far as they could see was a lush sea of waving grass, dotted with flowers of various colors and scents.

"Yes. It appears that our lands are in different seasons," Frinz explained.

Crystal knelt and touched the petal of a flower at her feet.

Brant watched Crystal with a tender expression. "Spring is her favorite season. It's when she shines the most."

Indeed, thought Frinz, *that is very true, but so do you Brant.*

Crystal stood up, dusting blades of grass from her legs. "Which way are we going?"

Frinz pulled out a handmade map from her cloak, unrolled it, and laid it on the ground.

"We are here," she said pointing to a blue dot on the map, "and here is the Ancient Library." Frinz pointed to a dot on the map, southeast of the Stone of Power. "If we keep a steady pace, we should reach the Ancient Library by sundown."

"Well that's good. It won't take long…just a few hours," Brant said.

"But, like the seasons, the times between our lands are indeed different. In your world it was late in the day, while in Thurnangl it is only morning," Frinz said with a small laugh.

There was a moment of silence before Crystal piped up, a smile on her face, "Well, I guess we should get walking then." She fell on her back and rolled down the grassy hill.

"See?" Brant said, as he too rolled down the hill.

Frinz smiled and whispered, "This is going to be great fun."

The trio walked through the tall field, the wind running its gentle fingers through their hair. It was rather difficult to walk through the waist-high grass, and they kept a careful watch with each step. Frinz cast a spell to cover any of their tracks along the way. As Crystal and Brant told stories of their childhood, Frinz was amazed by their perspective on the world. Crystal and Brant saw much more of the joys in life than the sorrows, much more than anyone she had ever met.

They continued on their trek, looking about them as small eyes and ears peeked through the tall grass. Crystal squealed with delight as the tiny creatures inched closer. A six legged animal with red fur as soft as silk nudged her leg affectionately, its large ears twitching as it purred. It scurried off as quickly as it came. A few colorful birds flew gracefully above. Their feathers almost sparkled in the sunlight. Around midday, the travelers stopped to rest. Frinz opened the satchel at her waist, revealing a loaf of bread, and divided it into three even pieces.

The bread was soft and delicious, and as they took their first bite, Crystal and Brant exclaimed together, "This is amazing!"

"You sound as though you have never eaten bread before," Frinz laughed.

"Well, we haven't had bread as good as this," said Brant, smiling as he took another bite.

"Who made it?" Crystal asked, as she inhaled the last delicious morsel.

"My mother baked it out of wheat honey and soft salnoom flower from my home in the mountains."

"So, are there lots of rare herbs in the mountains?" Brant asked, taking Crystal's hand as they stood to continue their journey.

"Oh yes! Herbs are plentiful all over our land, but in order to use them, you have to pick them the correctly. If you do not, then the herb will taste rather foul."

"Are there many kinds of animals living in Thurnangl?" Crystal asked, recalling visions of colorful creatures in her dreams.

Frinz let out a hearty laugh. "There are too many to count. They fill our land—hiding in every patch of grass, and nesting in every tree. You cannot walk far in a town before you find a colorful creature of some sort. In fact, I have a dear lifelong friend who is a dragon. Her name is Zabrina, and she lives in the mountains with me. She and I are close in age, so we grew up together. I met her when I was only a small child. My mother was picking herbs around our home and took me along with her. She says I was by her side one moment, and the next I was gone. She called to me, and when she finally found me, I was carrying a hatchling dragon. I thought I held a shimmering stone but was surprised to find it was a dragon egg. My mother and I were both astonished. We believed all the dragons to have fled long ago. We took the lonely dragon into our home, and she became family. Zabrina and I played together well and she was always gentle, even as she grew larger than me."

"What happened to her parents?" Brant asked.

Frinz began thoughtfully, "Long ago, just a few years after the war began, the dragons fled. They thought that a war would be unwise and only cause death. We believe Zabrina's egg lay dormant, waiting for us to find her. Now, only five dragons remain. In Thurnangl, Zabrina guards the mountains near my home. The forest of Mangü is protected by Drinin, a solitary dragon residing deep in the heart of the woods. Little is known of Drinin, but he is honored for his service to the forest creatures.

"Three dragons reside in Garzula serving Sörnam in his quest for destruction. Angerwin is a red dragon known for her strength and unique blue fire, and Hallin is a young dragon of very little experience who poses less threat than his counterparts. Calina serves as Sörnam's great weapon, using her age and wisdom to provide him knowledge and counsel."

When Frinz was finished she pointed to a tiny speck on the horizon. "We have arrived at the Ancient Library."

As Crystal and Brant grew nearer they noticed the structure was extremely small, merely a windowless, one-story hut. Upon closer inspection, they noticed that the door had no handle or knob.

Frinz placed her had on the door and whispered, "Fentorn Atrono Lenda."

The door swung open revealing a small room, in the center of which stood a silver spiral staircase that appeared to lead underground. As they descended the staircase, they saw a vast library spread out beneath them. The Ancient Library was a massive cathedral of knowledge with giant shelves rising to meet the forty-foot ceilings. Books of every shape and size lined the miles of shelves and flew from space to space, enchanted to reshelf themselves. Torches lined the ends of the bookcases and reflected off the silver floors, enhancing the magical feel of the enchanted space. Brooms swept the floors while the library ladders moved back and forth on the bookshelves, helping the books find their rightful places. At the library's center towered a magnificent clock surrounded by huge floating bowls of strange, colored liquid. The ceiling above reflected the sky outside the library walls. Stars shone brightly against a backdrop of darkness. The travelers were met by the hum of the library's magic as they descended the stairs.

Crystal and Brant took the last step from the spiral staircase and looked around with eyes of wonder.

"Wow! This is incredible!" Brant said.

Frinz beamed with pride.

A young woman peered suddenly around the corner of a book shelf, blinking through owl-like spectacles. In age and stature, she was much like Frinz, but her looks were decidedly different. Hair the color of straw hung straight to her shoulders, framing her face and accentuating the very unique burgundy hue of her eyes. At the sight of Frinz, the girl leapt from her hiding spot and straight into her friend's arms, nearly toppling them both.

"Frinz, I am overjoyed to see you!" she said gleefully.

When the woman noticed Crystal and Brant her smile brightened as she drank in the sight of them. Frinz was quick to introduce them.

"Crystal, Brant, I would like you to meet Liane, one of my very best friends. Liane's father was the one who found this library and brought hope back to our land. She is now the keeper of the library's knowledge. She has found many secrets within the Prophecy and will help us on our journey. Liane, I would like you to meet Crystal and Brant."

Liane bowed respectfully and said, "It is a great honor to meet you both."

Glancing at one another, Crystal and Brant bowed back courteously.

Liane studied the pair closely for a moment. "They look just as I had indeed imagined them. I can sense that their bond is already very strong."

"Bond?" asked Brant.

Liane paused, a look of puzzlement etched across her face, then smiled and beckoned to the pair. "Follow me, please."

Liane led the way as she answered Brant's question. "The bond I speak of is the magical connection you, Crystal and Brant, are said to share. As you continue through your lives together, your bond will grow exceptionally and carry from this life into the next. The bond is powerful and allows you to share each other's emotion, pain, worries, and needs. Think of it as a string connecting your hearts for all time."

Crystal and Brant exchanged looks of awe as they considered the weight of Liane's words. They had felt very close their entire lives but never paid it much mind to anything other than their incredible friendship. You could almost hear their hearts skip a beat.

Liane led the way to the southern end of the Ancient Library. There, on the wall, hung a prophecy as ancient as Thurnangl itself. The Prophecy scroll hung majestically from floor to ceiling, its vast area covering much of the wall. Inscribed on its crimson fabric, in gold thread, were words in a language foreign to Crystal and Brant.

"I believe Frinz has explained the Prophecy to you both?" Liane asked.

The teens nodded and Crystal added, "She explained that we have to use powers that we have…or get…or something… to end the civil war."

"Yes," Liane confirmed, "but first you must unlock your powers, and to do so, you must look inside your heart." Liane stepped closer to the scroll, ushering them to follow. Crystal and Brant stepped closer as Liane pulled a magnifying glass from her pocket and handed it to Brant. Leaning closely together, Crystal and Brant studied the scroll. Between the lines of the Prophecy were microscopic words, unseen to a naked eye.

"Those hidden words tell us of many secret books in the Ancient Library which explain how you both shall unlock your powers and continue to enhance them. The text speaks also of many other books in this very library that contain spells and incantations that are best for none to read. So I keep them locked away." Liane paused for a moment, looking to Frinz. "It seems that Frinz has neglected to explain many things to you. Why is that, my dear friend?"

Frinz ran her fingers through her hair nervously and explained, "You see, we had to depart quickly, and there was little time to explain."

Liane sighed and shook her head. "Frinz, you know as well as I that explanation and information must be our first priority. Action without knowledge will surely lead to disaster."

Frinz cast a worried glance toward her charges and whispered into Liane's ear, "I shall explain tonight while they rest."

Liane nodded and smiled at Crystal and Brant. "The first thing we must do is unlock your abilities."

The two blinked. "Now?" Brant asked.

"Yes. Yes. Crystal shall go first, as water and air are tranquil, uncomplicated, free-moving elements. Earth and fire pose a greater challenge, as they are unyielding elements. You both have separate paths to unlocking each element, but first we shall unlock your hearts. To do this, you must both let go of fear and worry. Crystal, let's proceed."

Liane paused as Crystal stepped forward and took a deep breath. "Close your eyes and think of the thing you fear most. Try to imagine the fear in tangible form. You need not share your fear with us, only visualize it for yourself."

Crystal did as Liane instructed and thought of her fear. The fear residing in the depths of her heart was losing her dearest friend, Brant. She was terrified that he would be harmed, ripped from her grasp, never to be seen again. The very thought made her heart race with anxiety.

"Now, Crystal, you need to conquer it. If you cannot overcome your fear, you cannot truly open your heart to the power that awaits you."

Crystal took another deep breath and reassured herself, *No that will never happen so long as I am alive no one will hurt Brant. I will protect him with all that I am! Brant is strong and so am I. I know we can accomplish anything together. Everything will be fine as long as we fight together.*

Crystal felt awash with peace, as her body relaxed, and her anxiety melted away. She opened her eyes, smiling at Liane.

"Now that you have unlocked your heart, you must find your powers. Inside every person's heart, there is power, but you must find it within yourself and learn to use it. For you to locate your powers, to control water and air, you must search deep within. All you have to do is close your eyes and see what your heart holds for you. Let the answer unfold and wash over you as wind and waves."

Crystal closed her eyes once more and searched deep within. After a few minutes of complete silence, Crystal felt the ground under her feet give way as though she were falling. She opened her eyes to find she was on a white sand beach. She felt the heat of the sun on her face, and the ripple of a sea breeze tickled her hair. The sound of waves filled her ears as she breathed in the crisp fresh air. The sensation passed quickly, but as Crystal's feet hit the ground once more, she knew she was forever changed. The sounds of the library surrounded her once more, and Crystal opened her eyes, smiling. She was determined. She was a warrior.

Liane smiled and patted Crystal's head, "Very good, Crystal, very good indeed."

Crystal looked at Brant, noticing worry etched across his face, and whispered, "Don't worry. It's not as hard as it seems."

Brant stepped forward as Liane turned to address him.

"Brant, your ability to control the elements earth and fire can only manifest once you, like Crystal, let go of fear. For, if your heart is full of worry, it will be locked to the magic within."

Brant took a deep breath and closed his eyes. He knew his fear well, as it rarely left him. He lived in terror of losing Crystal. If she were to be hurt, he wouldn't know to continue. Through his thoughts, he heard Liane's voice. "Now, find a solution, and release your fear."

No, Brant Thought, *I will never let that happen. I will protect Crystal with my entire being, no matter what the cost. I know she is strong, and so am I. Together, we can accomplish anything.* Relief settled over Brant, and grinning, he opened his eyes to meet Crystal's beaming gaze.

Liane continued, "Now, Brant, you must release your powers by channeling the strength within your heart."

As Brant closed his eyes, he felt stillness settle around him. He shifted uneasily and, for the briefest of moments, found himself standing atop a mountain, looking down on volcanic rock spewing forth heat and power into the air around him. The earth shook furiously as the fire below him pressed against his skin, but Brant stood tall, feeling no pain. Just as suddenly, he found himself back in the library.

Brant turned to Crystal and smiled. *Now I know I have the power to protect her.*

"You have both unlocked your abilities. Together, you control the four elements." Liane looked at Crystal and Brant standing before her, tears of pride gleaming behind her spectacles. She knew they had unlocked more than their individual powers. Together, they had paved the way for Thurnangl's salvation.

"Remember," Liane said, "with your powers come the added abilities, as well. Crystal, you possess magical healing powers, and Brant, your swordsmanship will be unmatched in all the lands. As your journey progresses, so too will your powers and abilities. Now, we must begin your training so that you may master each component of your newfound magic."

"Does it matter which element we learn first?" Brant asked.

"Yes, we will begin by mastering the element which each of you first unlocked." Liane turned and led them to the eastern end of the Ancient Library.

"Liane?" Crystal asked.

"Yes, Crystal?"

"Where did all of these books come from? There has to be thousands of them!"

Liane laughed under her breath, "Not much is known about them. From reading the text myself, I have discovered that this land was once plentiful, teaming with magnificent creatures like the dragons and the Entremdor, an incredible and magical race. Thurnangl was a beautiful and peaceful place. Then, many of the Entremdor were suddenly struck with an unknown and incurable illness. The disease took control of them, twisting them, body and soul. It spread to the land around them and left Thurnangl in ruin, a barren wasteland of death. The uninfected Entremdor battled the sick, banishing them far away in a deep canyon, before fleeing to The Forest of Mangö. There they hid, living deep behind the towering trees. As war continued to ravage the land, the Entremdor turned their backs on the people of Thurnangl, unwilling to feel further loss."

Crystal's heart ached for the people and for the land that was forsaken. Simply nodding, Crystal turned her attention to the incredible collection of books surrounding them. The trek through rows and rows of books seemed endless, but they finally reached their destination. Liane had brought them to her living area in the library—her home away from home. Nestled in the corner of the vast library was a small apartment, much like a cottage.

"It's so incredible that you live here!" Crystal exclaimed.

"Yes I found this small area in the Ancient Library when I was young, so when I was old enough, I left home and came here. I knew my mother would not mind, for she was busy raising my five younger siblings. Though, I do return home now and again to visit."

"What about your father?" Brant asked hesitantly.

"My father is away fighting the war, making plans for our great attack, but that is not for some time. For now, we must keep you both a secret."

Crystal wondered why they should be kept secret, but her thoughts were interrupted by her fatigue. Simultaneously, Crystal and Brant let out a massive yawn. Glancing at each other, they dissolved into laughter.

"Quit copying me Crystal. Gosh." Brant said teasingly.

"You both must be exhausted. Frinz can rest in the extra room, but would you two mind if you slept on the sofas? "Liane asked.

They didn't mind. After all they had seen and experienced in just one day's time, they were exhausted enough to sleep anywhere. Frinz left them on the sofa so that she and Liane could speak in private. Crystal and Brant settled into their makeshift beds and spoke quietly.

Crystal laughed, and Brant asked, "What's so funny?"

"Nothing, I just have a feeling all of this is going to be fun," Crystal said.

Brant smiled, and they both fell into a well-deserved slumber.

Frinz closed the door quietly and turned to Liane. "I must apologize. Since beginning this journey, I have felt as though someone, or something, was watching me. I did not want to take any chances with Crystal and Brant, especially knowing this was the very fate which befell my father."

"But Frinz, so few people know about the purpose of your journey."

Frinz sighed. "True, and yet I am still concerned. The length of our trip matters not, but I must keep them safe."

Liane took off her spectacles and looked deeply into Frinz's eyes, "You know that this journey will not be easy."

"Yes, Liane, I know this. You know that nothing is going to stop me. I will protect them with my life. For, without them, we are lost."

CHAPTER 4
THE JOURNEY AWAITS

Crystal woke early the next morning, the excitement of the previous day still present in her mind. As she stretched her limbs awake, Liane entered the room. In her arms, she held a number of books and peculiar objects.

"Good morning," Liane said softly.

Crystal rose, rubbing the sleep from her eyes, and whispered, "Good morning."

"Would you care to join me?" Liane asked in a hushed voice so that the others would not wake.

"Yes, I would love to join you!" Crystal answered excitedly. She readied herself quickly and joined Liane.

The Ancient Library was quiet as they made their way toward its center, as though it had not yet awakened to the new day. Liane inspected a bowl hovering near the great clock at the Library's center. Smiling with satisfaction, she dropped what appeared to be dried herbs into the bubbling concoction.

Crystal was struck by the delicious scents surrounding her and realized they reminded her of home, of her mother.

"Liane, why does the library smell like apple pie?"

Liane laughed, "Well, you see, the Library smells different to every person. It takes on the scent of their favorite memory or moment. For me it smells like my mother's home."

Brant tiptoed quietly behind Crystal until he was directly behind her. Without warning, he tapped her on the shoulder. Crystal jumped, letting out a shriek of fright. When she turned to see Brant laughing, she hit his arm playfully, frowning in consternation.

"Don't you ever do that again! You scared me."

Brant laughed and rubbed his arm. "You know I'll do it again, Crystal," he teased. "You were talking about the Library smelling like someone's favorite smell or memory, right? To me, it smells like my mother's brownies—the ones she always made for me when we were little."

"Yeah, your mother makes the best brownies," Crystal replied with a giggle.

Liane looked on, smiling knowingly as she spoke to Crystal. "Your aura, it sparkles and gleams with joy. And Brant's is that of someone filled with much happiness. It is astonishing seeing the mirror-like effect you have on one another."

"What's aura?" Brant asked curiously.

"Aura is a distinctive, but intangible, atmosphere that surrounds a person or object. Every wizard and witch has the ability to sense aura."

"That's unbelievable," Crystal said, her eyes lighting up with wonder.

"So, what are you doing?" Brant asked Liane, looking at the numerous objects she'd brought from her living quarters.

"I am creating a potion to pause the aging process while you are with us in Thurnangl. With it, you will cease aging until your quest is complete and you have returned home. It is unknown how long this quest will take, but when it does and you return to your home, we do not want to interrupt the world you left behind. I have brought with me a collection of sacred books that stay hidden from others, both friend and foe. These most powerful spells can cause great prosperity and great tragedy. There are spells of immortality, of protection, teleportation, even spells of death. I have made notes, transcribing Death Spells Sörnam, himself, created. I have been charged with protecting their secrets from the world, and so I shall," Liane explained.

"What is a death spell?" asked Crystal.

Liane sighed, the pain apparent in her eyes, "Death spells are the darkest of magic. They kill instantly and scar the mind and soul of those who use them. It is forbidden to practice such magic in Thurnangl, but Sörnam rules through fear and death. His people fight amongst themselves, and the lands of Garzula are filled with the cries of death spells."

Liane continued on with her work, dropping odd looking ingredients into the potion until it bubbled and swirled in the pot.

"Um, are we going to drink this?" Brant asked, suppressing a small gag at the site of the bubbling liquid.

"Yes," Liane replied with amusement, as she as she poured the brew into matching cups made of bone.

Crystal's face turned green, and Brant thought he might vomit.

Taking the mugs, they looked at each other once more and drank the questionable liquid.

"Mine tastes like brownies," Crystal said in surprise.

"Mine tastes like apple pie," said Brant.

They both burst into uncontrollable laughter, and Liane joined in.

As their mirth subsided, Liane spoke, studying them with great pride in her heart. "I have spent years in this library reading all manner of texts and growing more knowledgeable with each page, but I do not think I shall ever understand something as magical as your bond. You must cherish that bond and always hold it close."

"Liane, can Brant and I use magic?" Crystal asked suddenly. She could feel an unexplainable anticipation deep inside her heart.

"No. I am afraid that neither of you can cast spells or create potions, but your powers are magic in themselves, so do not be dismayed," Liane explained, smiling at their innocence.

Frinz joined them in the center of the library carrying two backpacks which held bread and water for their journey.

"Good morning," Crystal and Brant said together.

She smiled and handed them their belongings. "I am afraid, if we do not hurry, it will not be morning for long."

"Frinz, what does the Ancient Library smell like to you?" Crystal asked curiously.

Frinz flushed and smiled a secretive smile "It smells like a person." Turning, she followed Liane to the silver spiral staircase.

Brant gazed questioningly at Crystal, but she shook her head. They would leave Frinz with her secret smiles, for now.

When they reached the silver staircase, Liane paused.

Reaching into her pocket, she revealed matching rings made of silver. The rings had been forged with great skill and care. An intricate setting had been created consisting of four thin bars rising to create a round cage, inside of which sat a tiny, black ball. As the ring moved with the hand that bore it, the bars caught the light, and the ball moved freely, creating a melodic jingling sound.

"These are for you. I made them last night. Whenever you lose each other, you have only to tap the ring, and you will be able to speak to one another."

"Thank you," they said together.

Crystal placed the ring on her left hand and Brant on his right.

Producing two beautiful cloaks of a thin material the color of summer sky, Liane continued, "It would be wise for you to have these, as well. They are worn, but their protection may come in handy during your travels."

"Oh how beautiful!" Crystal exclaimed with a laugh of delight.

Both Crystal and Brant thanked Liane again and began climbing the Library stairs.

Liane hugged Frinz and whispered, "You will watch over them, will you not?"

"Of course," Frinz reassured her dear friend, "it is my duty, just as it is yours to guard the knowledge contained within these walls, Liane."

They said goodbye, and the trio climbed the stairs to the building above.

Crystal and Brant turned to take one last look. Frinz answered their unspoken question, "Worry not. We will see her again."

Frinz rested her hand on the door and recited the incantation which opened it. The travelers took a step into the sunlight and toward the next leg of their journey.

CHAPTER 5
A CHILDHOOD LOST

"Where are we going now?" Crystal asked Frinz as they trekked through the tall grass, their footprints vanishing behind them.

"Our destination is the city of Meclen—a simple day's journey by foot."

The group plodded on through an ocean of green grass, kept cool by the gentle breeze that blew the clouds softly across the sky. Crystal glanced at the sky, wondering at her power to control water. She recalled, from science class, that water particles were everywhere, even in the air. *So,* she thought, *I could gather that water.*

Cupping her hands as she concentrated, Crystal took a breath. Slowly, her hands filled with water. Concentrating further, Crystal slowly pulled her hands apart and gasped as the water stayed afloat in midair. Moving the water through the air, she giggled in delight.

"What are you doing?" Brant asked.

"I'm collecting water, see?" Crystal splashed the water in his face, with a laugh.

"Don't make me throw this," Brant teased, as a small rock flew from the ground and into his upturned hand."

Crystal's jaw dropped. "How did you do that?"

"Well," he said, tossing the stone up in the air and catching it, "while you played with your water, I figured I would test my own powers."

They ate while they traveled, rarely stopping. As the day wore on, Crystal found herself able to collect larger amounts of water, while Brant manipulated a dozen small rocks at once. The afternoon brought boredom to the teens, who were not used to such long journeys. They were growing weary from the trek and had seen little to amuse them.

With a laugh, Crystal turned to Brant and tapped his shoulder playfully, "Tag! You're it!"

Brant ran after her with a gleeful smile.

Frinz smiled wistfully, pain mixing with pleasure at the sight.

They are playing a game as though they were children, she thought. *I have not played such games since I was small.*

Nodding in unison, the teens ran to Frinz and tapped her shoulder shouting, "You're it!"

They bounded away, laughing, but their merriment ceased when they realized she did not follow.

"Frinz, don't you want to play?" asked Brant.

"I think not. I am far too old to play games, and I believe so too might you be," she said, turning to continue on their path.

Too old?" Crystal asked in amazement. "You're never too old to have fun! Now, come on. You're it!

With a sly grin, Frinz turned and sprang after the youngsters. Their raucous laughter rang across the still, grassy plain.

Running, laughing, playing games, these are things I have not done for so long, Frinz thought. *For too long have I been absorbed in my lot as bearer of the ancient Prophecy. But, when I'm here with them, it seems as though I can forget it all. My thoughts just seem to drift away from the burdens that have weight them down for so long. These two are truly what Thurnangl needs.*

The play of the day proved to be a welcome diversion, and it was not long before the sun began its descent on the horizon. In the fading light, they could see a walled city and hear the bustling sounds of the people within.

"Hey what's that?" Crystal asked, panting a little from their activity.

"It seems we have reached our destination," advised Frinz. "I must warn you, the city of Meclen does not welcome strangers warmly. Our goal is to keep you hidden, for now. If the people were to know about your existence, you could be in great danger. You're still learning your powers, and I do not want an attack before you're ready. We shall rest, out of sight, for the night."

Setting down their blankets, the three travelers huddled around a cloaked fire, magically visible only to them. A silence fell, each lost in thought, recalling events of the past days. The crackle of the fire and coos of nighttime creatures filled their ears.

"I had such fun today," Frinz told her companions. She grew suddenly pensive, her eyes never leaving the fire. "I am afraid I have had little time for play these many years."

"Didn't you get to play games as a kid?" Brant asked. His heart ached as he sensed the sorrow behind her words.

Frinz's reply came only after a long pause. "My childhood was not a time of play. War has tainted the children of Thurnangl. I spent mine intent on carrying out my part in the Prophecy. Studying spells and incantations was my play. Perhaps I lost my childhood," Frinz pondered as her eyes moved, gazing at the dancing stars above, "but maybe that was part of my role in this greater purpose for which we fight."

Crystal smiled sympathetically. "I admire that. I believe that everything happens for a reason. Even if we can't see it now, it all falls together eventually."

Frinz returned the smile, and lay down on her blanket, "You are right. Sleep well tonight, Brant and Crystal, for when the sun awakens from its deep slumber, we will visit Meclen."

While the others slept deeply, Crystal stared at the star-studded sky, unable to calm her mind. The nighttime sounds and smells around her were foreign and unnerving. She smiled as she glanced at her friend sleeping soundly nearby. Brant could sleep through anything.

Idly, Crystal played with droplets of water, gathering them from the damp night air and moving them to and fro in a growing band which splashed on nearby rocks. A sudden and strange sensation pulsed through her arm, and Crystal looked down to find her water splayed on the ground. The nearest rock now bore a small, deep cut as though someone had slashed it with a blade. Astonished by her discovery, Crystal gathered her water and concentrated, making another mark, then another.

Crystal shook Brant's shoulder in excitement. "Brant, Brant! Wake up! I have to show you something!"

"Huh? What is it? I *was* asleep, you know," he said groggily.

"Yes, yes I know, but look!" she pointed to the scarred rock.

"So? It's a rock. What's so special about it?"

"No, look closer," Crystal said.

Brant moved forward, examining the stone carefully. Perplexed, he ran his fingers over the fresh grooves on its surface.

"So, you did this… with water?" Brant asked.

Crystal nodded with pride.

"Don't get too far ahead of me," Brant winked. They laughed together, and Crystal yawned, her mind finally relaxing.

Placing a hand on her shoulder, he continued, "We should both rest. It's going to be a long day tomorrow." Smiling, they both fell into a well-deserved sleep, ready to face whatever was in store come morning.

CHAPTER 6
A STEP TOO FAR

Brant woke with a start. *What a nightmare*, he thought.

Awakened by his distress, Crystal sat up, rubbing her eyes. "Are you ok?"

Brant mumbled in reply, "Just a bad dream."

"You want to talk about it? Maybe I can help," Crystal said, concern etched on her face.

Brant glanced toward Frinz, ensuring she was fast asleep before sharing his nightmare.

"Well, in my nightmare," he began, visions still swirling in his mind, "I was walking through the mountains, and it was dark and raining. Suddenly, I heard your voice in the distance, and it sounded like you were screaming. I couldn't reach you or contact you. Even the ring didn't work."

Brant paused, looking into Crystal's eyes, which mirrored his own fear. He nervously ran a hand through his hair. "As I searched for you, the screaming turned to crying, and I still couldn't find you. I woke up sure that I'd lost you. Not that you're weak," he added hurriedly.

Crystal let out a tiny laugh.

"I don't see how any of this is funny at all," he snapped.

"No." Crystal fiddled with her locket as if the trinket truly was her heart. "It's just that, when I was unlocking my elements and letting go of my fear…that fear was losing someone I care about very much."

The pair smiled knowingly at each other, and Crystal continued, her tone less serious. "I promise I will do my best to keep your dream from coming true and, of course, to make sure you stay out of trouble."

Brant replied with a laugh, "I'm sure you'll find trouble somehow."

"Me? Trouble?" asked Crystal innocently.

"Well you said it first," Brant teased as they laughed together.

Frinz laid awake, listening to the pair and fearing the worst ahead. They were her responsibility, hers to protect.

What if I can't? she wondered in fear.

Her thoughts were interrupted by Crystal's voice. "I don't think we need to worry. We've got each other…and Frinz too."

Frinz smiled and sat up, unseen by the teens, shaking off her worry.

"I feel like Frinz is a sister," Crystal continued. "She's so kind and protective. I can tell she truly cares about us."

"Really?" Frinz asked warmly, startling her companions. Crystal's face grew crimson with embarrassment.

"Yes, you are so very nice and protective, just as a sister would be," Crystal said kindly.

"Thank you," said Frinz, overcome by the sentiment. "That means the world to me." She rose to her feet, beckoning the others. "We should make our way to Meclen while its people still sleep. We'll need to purchase new garments so that you might better blend in."

Gathering their belongings, they started toward the city.

As the travelers approached the city gates, Frinz donned the hood of her cloak and motioned for Brant and Crystal to do the same. Ahead, two guards dozed at their posts, leaving the path into Meclen open.

"Keep to the shadows as best you can," whispered Frinz. "The sun shall not rise for some time, favoring our travels. Keep close, and tell no one your names."

Nodding their agreement, Crystal and Brant followed Frinz through the city gates. Though the streets were quiet, the few folks up and about stared openly at the strangers. Instinctively, Crystal and Brant moved closer together.

"I don't like this," Crystal whispered.

The trio made their way through the vast city, winding down alleyways and behind shops. Despite their brisk pace, they had not reached their destination before the full hustle and bustle of the day began. As more and more people flooded the streets, they struggled to stay together and inconspicuous. Midday brought them to a halt in front of a small shop.

"Wait here," Frinz instructed, "I'll go inside to purchase supplies. You must stay out of sight as best you can."

Brant and Crystal waited obediently for Frinz, but as the minutes wore on, their patience waned. Crystal spotted a cart full of exotic fruits unlike anything she'd seen before, and her curiosity got the best of her.

"Brant! Look at all the strange, colorful fruit. C'mon! Let's check it out!" Crystal said excitedly.

Brant watched Crystal walk toward the cart. His better judgment told him to stop her.

"Don't worry," Crystal called back to him, "it's not far, and we can still see the shop!"

Brant sighed, giving in. He would stay within view of the shop door and all would be well, he was sure.

The cart held a vast array of fruits in every size, color, and texture. Wondering at the foreign produce, Brant examined a spikey, green fruit closely, turning it about in his hand. The fruit was suddenly knocked from his grasp as the owner of the fruit cart grabbed Brant's wrist and yelled, "HA! Thought you and your little band of thieves could steal from me again, did you?"

Nearby, Crystal heard the commotion, and her eyes met Brant's.

"No! Please you don't understand," Brant began, falling silent as the man brandished a sharpened spear.

"You and your little friends are going to pay for the food you have stolen!"

Brant protested, shaking in fear as the man's grip tightened around his wrist, "I don't know what you're talking about! I'm not a thief. I wasn't going to—"

"Do not mess with me boy. The Stone of Power has granted me the gift of strength. Though it is a common gift, it provides me the power to break you in half!"

Brant heard his bones crack and knew his wrist was broken.

Crystal felt her friend's agony and acted without thought. With little more than a flick of her hand, she had collected water into a thin whip which sliced through the cart owner's spear shaft. The spear tip clattered to the ground, and the man stepped back, aghast. He stared, first in horror and then recognition, at the girl with her outstretched hand, whose hood had fallen to her shoulders.

The crowd backed away in fright, and the cart owner ripped his hand from Brant's wrist as though he'd been burned. Frinz took in the scene as she stepped out of the shop.

"Oh no," she said softly.

The crowd erupted in whispers which grew steadily into the roar of an angry mob. A voice yelled loudly above the others, "Quick! Grab them before they escape!" and the mob surged forward. Without a second thought, Crystal seized Brant's uninjured hand and ran. With a sigh, Frinz pulled her hood tighter and dissolved into the dark alley, doing her best to go unnoticed by the crowds.

Crystal and Brant wound through the streets, running as fast as their feet could carry them. They found their way suddenly blocked by a wall and were forced to choose a new direction. Looking left and then right, they shouted, "This Way!" together and dashed off in opposite directions.

Brant ran until he could go no further. Stumbling into a small alley, he collapsed against the wall. His wrist throbbed violently, and Brant saw that it was swollen and horribly discolored.

"I wish you had mastered your healing powers, Crystal. They would come in handy right about now." Brant looked around for his friend, but she was nowhere in sight.

Remembering the fork in the path and his decision to run, Brant sighed with frustration. The ring on his finger jingled suddenly, the bars on it opening to release the tiny ball inside. As the ball rose into the air, it flattened into a disc and flickered, before displaying Crystal's face.

"Where are you?" she asked in a whisper. Brant looked around the corner and saw the nearest street sign.

"I'm behind Gendor Street."

"Ok, I'm on my way. Don't move." Crystal's face disappeared, and the disc reverted to its original form, sinking back into the ring.

"Like I'm going anywhere." Brant said sarcastically into the emptiness around him.

Crystal found that she was further away from Brant than she had anticipated. When she finally found him, she was out of breath from her search.

"I...thought...I would...never...find...you," she panted.

Even as she spoke, Crystal examined Brant's injured wrist, touching it delicately. "I'm sorry. I wish so much that I could heal your arm, even a little."

At her touch, Brant felt his wrist grow cold and watched as the swelling and discoloration subsided slightly. It was still broken, but not as badly.

"It looks like you got your wish," Brant breathed with a sigh of relief.

They were startled by the sudden appearance of a bright ball of light advancing toward them. Crystal and Brant jumped to their feet, preparing for the worst. The light faded, revealing a welcome sight.

"Frinz!" they said together.

"How did you find us?" Brant asked.

"I used a location orb," Frinz explained, "It can locate anyone I need to find. An ancient spell from the Library, which only I know."

Crystal's pleasure in seeing her friends again dissolved quickly as she recalled her role in their current situation. Eyes brimming, Crystal turned to her companions.

"I'm so sorry. I've doomed us." Unable to continue, Crystal dissolved into tears.

Frinz gave a tiny smile and placed a hand on the sobbing girl's shoulder. "There is little to be done about what has passed. All that matters is your safety. Now, let us find a way out of this wretched city."

Reaching under her cloak, Frinz produced a tiny whistle hanging from a beautiful silver chain around her neck. She took a deep breath, blowing through the whistle, but no sound was heard. When she finished, Frinz smiled in satisfaction.

"Good," she said, "We must move quickly lest we be spotted. The townspeople are certain to be looking for you. We will move toward the easternmost part of the city where there are few people to spot you."

There escape from the city was tedious and made longer by their need to stay hidden. When finally they made their way past the far gates and into the safety of the fields, the sun was setting low in the sky. Brant, able once more to speak aloud, asked, "What did that broken whistle do anyway?"

His question was answered immediately by a deafening roar from above. Looking up at the darkening sky, they saw a flash of silver wings, and a dragon flew overhead. Gracefully, it turned in the air and landed next to the group, drawing in its wings and lowering its massive head. The dragon's length extended twenty-five feet from nose to tail, and it stood eight feet tall with steely scales of shimmering silver. Frinz ran forward and embraced the great dragon. "Zabrina! How I have missed you!"

"And I you, my dear friend." The dragon spoke in a rich, gentle voice, startling Crystal and Brant.

The mighty dragon examined Frinz's companions with wise, silver eyes before addressing them. "Hello, Brant and Crystal. It is indeed a great honor to meet you both."

Zabrina bowed her head, and the teens returned the gesture. Crystal stepped forward, running her fingers along the dragon's warm, smooth scales. Being so near the magnificent creature seemed to calm Crystal's nerves and relieve her fears. As Brant moved toward Zabrina, his wrist healed itself, the pain and swelling disappearing completely. He looked at her questioningly.

"I am a healer," Zabrina explained. "That is, my aura has healing qualities that I may bestow upon those I choose. I shall teach Crystal to heal when the time comes, but other matters are now at hand. We must leave quickly, for the people of the city will surely be drawn to the sight of a dragon such as me."

Frinz climbed on Zabrina's back and offered her hand to the duo.

"Come. Climb on," Frinz urged.

Crystal and Brant looked at each other in astonishment. Brant grasped Frinz's hand and allowed her to hoist him onto Zabrina's back. Crystal followed.

"Hold tight," Zabrina instructed as she unfurled her wings. She launched herself from the ground and flew into the night sky.

Crystal watched the lights of Meclen fade into the distance as they flew steadily onward toward new adventures. Turning her back on the city that had brought them such trouble, Crystal smiled at Brant. Thoughts turned into dreams as the dragon's wings lulled them into a deep sleep filled with shared visions of what was to come.

CHAPTER 7

MAGIC IS A WONDERFUL THING

That night was a peaceful one for the trio riding on the back of the mighty dragon, Zabrina. As Crystal and Brant slept soundly, Frinz told her dear friend of all that had transpired during their time apart. Zabrina heard the smile in Frinz's voice as she described her adventures with their companions.

"Is that a smile, dear friend?" the dragon asked with a chuckle. "You have not smiled that brightly in so long, but aren't such smiles usually reserved for a special someone?"

Frinz was grateful the dark of night hid her blushing face. She turned to the two sleeping figures behind her.

"Crystal and Brant are such beacons of light in the midst of this darkness. Their joy spreads to those around them." Frinz's look turned somber as she continued. "I do fear that their innocence leaves them ill prepared for what lies ahead."

"Worry not," Zabrina reassured, "for they possess wisdom beyond their years. Their story is written, their parts assigned. They will lead us in victory."

"Yes," Frinz said, hugging Zabrina's neck. "We must trust in our new heroes. We must trust in the Prophecy."

Frinz succumbed to her weariness and was soon sleeping soundly as Zabrina flew on through the quiet night. Their journey continued through the night. Crystal, Brant, and Frinz slept peacefully on the mighty dragon's back until they were awakened by the first rays of morning sunlight over the mountaintops. The travelers took in the beauty of dawn, appreciating its stillness after the excitement of the previous day.

Crystal and Brant gazed down from their perch to find a flock of birds gliding gracefully below. They gasped in amazement at the beautiful sight before the birds dissolved into the air, as if by magic. Frinz laughed at their surprise as she explained the camouflaging nature of the flock and its ability to take on the properties and color of the scenery around it. Brant smiled at Crystal. The land from their dreams was truly a wondrous place.

The sun shone brightly above them when Zabrina announced that they would be landing. Brant and Crystal gazed below to see mountains, covered in dense forest, spreading as far as they could see. Frinz cast a quick spell, bending the trees to clear a path for the great dragon's landing. Zabrina drew in her stunning wings and landed softly. Crystal looked in astonishment at the massive trees towering once move above them. The travelers slid from Zabrina's back excitedly. Crystal and Brant clasped hands, steadying each other as they regained their balance.

Out of the corner of Crystal's eye she saw a black bird land in a tree not far from where they stood. With feathers blacker than the darkest night and piercing eyes of onyx, the bird was as magnificent as it was terrifying. She watched as the bird studied her, as though it were taking in every detail.

"Come on, Crystal," Brant said taking her hand. "If we stay back here we'll get lost."

Shaken from her reverie, Crystal let Brant lead her forward. She glanced back to the branch where the bird had been, but it had vanished.

The vast forest was a place of comfort to the travelers. Brant and Crystal felt themselves relaxing as though the trees were protecting them. Along their path, they met with all manner of strange and wondrous creatures. Blinking eyes stared at them from the trees, and animals of every color and size followed them as they journeyed forth.

Crystal stopped short at the site of a four-armed animal with the largest ears she had ever seen. It cooed to her as if inviting her closer, but when it turned, she could see dangerous spikes of deep crimson lining its back.

Halting with Crystal, Brant pointed and asked, "Frinz, what's that?"

"That is an aquentaro," Frinz answered, as the creature jumped from its perch, landing at their feet.

Brant knelt, extending his arm as though to pet the exotic beast. "Stop!" Zabrina cried, jumping forward. "The aquentaro is the deadliest of creatures. One touch of its spikes will kill even the largest enemy!"

Brant continued forward, undeterred by Zabrina's warning. The aquentaro nuzzled his hand, cooing in delight, and Brant laughed.

Zabrina and Frinz looked on in wonder as Crystal explained, "Brant has always had a way with animals."

Frinz laughed in relief as she watched the fierce creature fight for Brant's attention. "It seems Brant's talent for taming beasts extends to the creatures of Thurnangl." Brant lightly blushed in modest protest. "Come," Frinz continued, "We must continue on, for we are almost to our destination."

They bid their new friend goodbye and continued on their way, stopping every so often to point out the curious creatures they encountered. Creatures lined their path and met them at every turn, as though welcoming them to the forest. Birds of every imaginable size and shape swooped in greeting, some landing briefly, as though bowing to the group. Mesmerized by the forest inhabitants, Crystal and Brant did not notice that their guides had stopped walking until they collided with her.

"Why did we stop?" Crystal asked.

Beaming, Frinz answered, "We have arrived."

Before them, in a small clearing, stood the ruins of a house, long burned and deserted. A blackened door stood as the only intact part of what might once have been a beautiful cottage. Its golden doorknob shone brightly, out of place in the charred remains.

"Where is 'here,' exactly?" Brant asked.

"Home," Frinz said, turning the doorknob.

The door opened to reveal a vast hallway of fiery orange. Crystal and Brant stared speechlessly at what had, only moments before, been the burned shell of a home. They gave a collective gasp as Zabrina stepped through the tiny doorway, and it expanded to accommodate her size. They made their way down the hall, following the scent of sweet treats and the sound of busy hands at work.

"Mother, we are home!" Frinz called, her voice echoing down the passageway.

A lovely woman appeared in the passage, wiping her hands on the apron around her waist. She was a tiny woman, standing slightly taller than Frinz, with eyes of the same deep lavender. Her golden hair framed her face, just reaching her ears. She wore a gown the color of buttercups, which flowed to just below her knees, as though she were wearing summer. At the sight of Frinz, she ran forward, embracing the younger woman fiercely.

"I was so worried about you!" she cried. "When Zabrina left, I thought something terrible happened."

"Worry no more, Mardra. We are all home." Zabrina nudged the golden lady gently with her snout.

Mardra released Frinz and, beaming, turned to Crystal and Brant.

"They look just as I imagined. Hello, Crystal and Brant, it is a great honor to finally meet you."

"Nice to meet you," Brant and Crystal said together.

Mardra's brow furrowed as she spied the open door behind them. "An open door invites danger. We must honor the house and the protection it provides." She snapped her fingers, and the door shut firmly.

Crystal's attention was caught by the door's engraving. It bore the figure of a man, standing nobly with his sword in the air. The man's face was kind, yet the eyes held a bold fierceness, as though this man stood guard, protecting those he loved from the greatest of evils.

"Who is that on the door?" Crystal asked.

"Ah, that is my dear husband, Malchior—Frinz's father."

Mardra paused for a moment, weighing her words, before continuing, "He stands there as he stood on the day of our betrothal, promising to be with me for all time. His words echo in my heart constantly. 'I promise, no matter what, that I shall let no harm come to you. Though my body may one day perish, my spirit shall linger on with you. We shall remain together, always.' His passing from this world did nothing to change his promise."

As Malchior's oath settled over them, the group grew silent. Brant met Crystal's gaze, and together they basked in the comfort of Malchior's protection. Here, they were safe. Here, they were protected.

The silence was broken by the sound of Crystal's stomach rumbling in hunger. She blushed and asked, "What smells so good?"

Mardra laughed and beckoned them forward. "Follow me, and I will show you."

Following their host, Crystal and Brant stepped into the enormous kitchen and were met with the most pleasant sights and scents imaginable. Mardra made her way to a large island in the center of the room, upon which sat the beginnings of a great feast. An enormous pantry made up the wall closest to the entryway, and shelves lined the remaining wall space. Two large ovens were warming all manner of delicious treats.

Zabrina made her way to the great fireplace at the far end of the room and immediately collapsed on the rug in front of it, exhausted from their journey.

Beyond the fireplace was a dining room, much like the banquet halls of the great kings one might read about in novels. A great oak table no less than thirty feet in length sat in the room's center. Brant counted twenty-five chairs sitting around the huge eating space. The dining room's walls were lined with cupboards, and a second fireplace sat along the farthest wall.

"Wow!" Crystal exclaimed in admiration.

"I don't even think the lunch room at our school is this big," Brant said.

"Why is the room so big if there are only three people living here?" Crystal asked.

"Here, our leaders convene to discuss great matters and hear from the people. For Thurnangl to thrive, it is important that all have a voice," Mardra explained.

Mardra turned to the stove to mutter a spell, and a bright light shone from the oven. A pan of perfectly golden muffins floated from the oven's mouth and landed softly on the counter.

"Incredible." Crystal breathed, taking a muffin from the tray.

Handing a muffin to Brant, Mardra beckoned them to follow. "Come. I will show you the rest of our home."

Crystal and Brant followed Mardra back to the entrance hall and through a set of barely visible doors. Through the doors stood a staircase, which led to the home's second story.

Answering the amazed looks of her guests, Mardra explained, "Magic allows us to manipulate space and use it as we need."

At her explanation, Crystal grew bold and asked, "Ms. Mardra, as we travelled into the woods and nearer to your house, I felt different, safer. Why is that?"

Mardra beckoned them forward as she explained. "The house and surrounding woods have been shielded from Sörnam's army and those who are unwelcomed. Though my husband's physical form has left this world, his spirit and magic linger, protecting all he held dear. None have found us, and none shall, with his protection."

They stopped in front of a large door. On it was an inscription and a large hand print. "Now," Mardra continued, "should you choose to enter this most secret of rooms, you must place your hand directly on the handprint, and the door will recognize your goodness and open."

As Mardra demonstrated, the door swung gently open revealing shelves upon shelves of books. Crystal was overwhelmed by the sheer volume of books at her disposal and stared, enthralled, at the shelves.

"Come, I would like to show you where you will be sleeping." Mardra led them back to the staircase and ascended further.

"These are our sleeping quarters. As you can see, we each have a separate bedroom. You shall sleep in this corridor as well. If you will go to the wall and place your hand like so," Mardra demonstrated as she spoke, reciting the incantation for them.

Following her example, Brant and Crystal each placed their left hand on the wall next to Mardra's. "Now," she continued, "close your eyes and picture your room, just as you would wish it to be. The room you need and desire will manifest before you, but you must picture it in your mind."

Following her instruction, the teens closed their eyes and thought hard about the rooms they desired. Opening their eyes, each placed a hand on the doorknob before them. Their doors opened to a shared room split down the middle only by the very different styles it had adopted to accommodate its inhabitants.

Brant's portion of the room was painted a bright, cheery red and accented by furniture in deep green. His bedding was a red that precisely matched the walls, and in the corner was a nightstand of marble, inlayed with fossils unlike any he had seen before. He opened his closet to find it filled with clothing in the style of the people of

Thurnangl, each piece a color that represented the fire and earth he could manipulate and possess. Glancing at the ceiling, he was thrilled by the visions of fire, flickering as though they would burn up the room.

As Brant marveled at the enchanted ceiling, Crystal was busy discovering the delights of her side of the shared bedroom. Her walls were the blue of the ocean, her bedding the color of a summer sky. On a wooden nightstand sat a fishbowl with tiny fish in every color, swimming contentedly. Her floor was carpeted in a soft white fleece which, like her dresser, sat like snow amidst a sea of sapphires. Opening her closet, she squealed in delight at the rows upon rows of frocks in every blue tone imaginable. She couldn't wait to don the gorgeous threads. Stepping from the closet, she glanced up to see an ocean above her with roiling waters and creatures of the deep darting to and fro.

When they'd had time to explore, Mardra said, "I do hope this room suits you both."

In answer, Brant and Crystal collapsed simultaneously onto their beds in delight. "Absolutely!"

CHAPTER 8

A BEDTIME STORY

Brant and Crystal lay in their beds, staring at the enchanted ceiling above and waiting for Mardra to call them to dinner.

"Crystal?" Brant asked, turning on his side.

"Yes," she said, still gazing at her ceiling.

"What do you think of all of this? I mean, now that we've had a chance to sit down and think, what's going through your head?"

Crystal paused to consider. Then, with a smile on her lips, she answered, "How many people get the chance to save a world? I think we're in for a big adventure."

Brant laughed. "I guess you're right. We're in for the ride of our lives, and I'm thinking 'Did we make the right choice?'"

"We just approach problems differently," Crystal replied. "You're the level-headed hero coming to the rescue, and I'm that silly girl who rushes in impulsively." With a humorless laugh, her smile dissolved into a frown.

"Try not to be so hard on yourself," Brant sighed, "but you are right about one thing. We're here, and we have the power to help. This is our chance to make a difference"

"Yeah!" Crystal jumped up from bed. "Come on, let's go help with dinner. I'll race you!"

Crystal dashed from the room as Brant yelled, "Hey, that's cheating!"

Scrambling to catch up, he lunged at Crystal as she reached the bottom of the stairs. They tumbled together, laughing. Their merriment ceased at the sound of Frinz's voice.

"I have had the feeling the whole of my journey, and it has not faltered. It's as though someone or something is following us. I rushed our travels to escape it, but it persists." Frinz played with her hair nervously as she spoke to her mother and Zabrina. "Something is very wrong." Frinz paused, uneasy.

Brant looked at Crystal only to see her face darkened with fear. They listened as Frinz continued.

"I can feel it in every bit of magic that flows through my body. I know not whether our enemy will strike, or if Raymond will make the first advance, but a blow is coming. We must be ready."

Sensing the teens' presence, Zabrina let out a small laugh. "Why are you hiding?" she asked. "Here, we do not speak words we wish unheard. You need not act secretly in this house."

Crystal and Brant fell from behind the wall with a dull thud, as Frinz and Mardra looked on, momentarily diverted from their troubles.

"Sorry," they said together.

"No need for apologies, my dears," Mardra reassured them, "For here, we share knowledge and thought."

Brant grasped Crystal's hand and led her to the fireplace where they sat down in unison. For a moment, the room was silent as the pair stared into the fire's gleaming embers. Flames licked at the solid gold frame bearing up a hearth which glistened with emeralds. Its warmth calmed Crystal and brought her comfort.

Crystal glanced questioningly at Frinz. "Who is Raymond? I know you mentioned him before, and I heard his name when we were in Meclen, as well."

"Raymond," Mardra answered, "is the Leader of our Army. He is one of the many Leaders of Thurnangl."

"Just how many leaders are there?" Brant asked, tearing his gaze away from the mesmerizing flames.

Mardra continued, "In our land, we believe that all are responsible for ruling. We have chosen The Ten Leaders of Thurnangl to care for our large matters, but no single person or group can decide how we are to live."

Brant continued his conversation with Mardra about Thurnangl's leaders, but Crystal caught Frinz's eye.

"What's the matter?" Crystal asked.

"Nothing, really," Frinz said patting Crystal's hand. "I will be fine."

Crystal stared deeply into Frinz's eyes until her friend's resolve crumbled. "I carry much guilt for the way our trip has unfolded," Frinz sighed.

"No-no you shouldn't apologize to me. I'M sorry!" Crystal exclaimed, pausing for a moment before continuing. "We can't dwell on our mistakes. If we constantly look behind us, we won't be able to find our way forward, and we'll fall. I can only promise to do my best, going forward. Won't you do the same?"

Frinz smiled affectionately at Crystal. She knew very few people who spoke words filled with such kindness.

"Yes," Frinz said, "Thank you, Crystal. Your heart is truly kind."

"We must begin dinner preparations" Mardra said, making her way to the kitchen.

"Brant, could you get some rootleaf from one of the living room cabinets, please?" Mardra asked.

Brant stood and asked, "Which cabinet?"

"Oh, it doesn't matter," Mardra replied.

Confused, Brant shrugged and proceeded to the living room. Examining the cabinets, he found them all empty. He thought it best to check once more, and opening the closest cabinet, was met with a small pile of root-shaped leaves.

But there was nothing there before?! Brant thought.

Brant took the handful of roots and walked back to the kitchen, baffled by what he had witnessed.

Mardra laughed at the confusion on his face. "I failed to mention that each cabinet in the house is linked to my needs. I was one of the two magic users who built this house, and it now provides me with that which I need, so long as we have it in stock."

Understanding a little more about the house and its abilities, Crystal and Brant set to work helping the others with dinner preparations. Brant played idly with a knife, letting his mind wander to thoughts of their adventures and of Crystal. He was surprised when the blade flew from his hands to hit the cupboard across the room.

"Brant?!" Crystal screeched. She stood with the knife only inches from her face.

"You should really control your powers better, Brant," she said teasingly.

Brant ripped the knife from the door and shook it in Crystal's face, but she simply laughed and walked away. The party's hard work paid off, and they soon sat at the great table with a feast before them.

"I think it is now time for you to see what truly goes on behind these walls." Zabrina's voice echoed through the immense dining room, as she raised her head to the ceiling and said, "Andorozen"

High above the table, a flat, black surface appeared.

"Long ago, our land was cured of a dreaded sickness by a great and powerful wizard named Ozu. He used his great power to find a land where witches and wizards could live without fear of persecution form non-magic folk. As a final gift, he sacrificed his life and provided us with a stone which held magic beyond compare. It would come to be known as The Stone of Power."

The black surface above the table showed the grassy hill where they had entered into the land before changing to a scene of people in every shape and size.

"The stone was hidden deep in the ground, and from its hiding place, it granted unique powers to the people in the land. Some were able to tame the most vicious creatures without uttering a word. Others could forge and wield magnificent weapons."

"Some were given great strength," Brant said, clenching his fist.

Zabrina nodded. "Yes. There are rather common gifts like that of strength or knowledge, but The Stone has granted many a unique and powerful gift as well."

The orb above them changed with Zabrina's words, showing brief snapshots of witches and wizards with amazing powers.

Zabrina continued. "A select few have much greater abilities. They may speak with beings we can neither see nor hear. These great powers made those with lesser or no gifts envious, and so their anger grew. Gone were sensible thoughts and reason. These jealous souls fled to Garzula, letting themselves be corrupted by their wish to possess what they could not.

"As their numbers grew in the land of Garzula, they amassed armies for a single purpose—destroy the Stone of Power and, with it, all great magic in our world. For over three hundred years they have sought the stone, waging war against those who would have peace. But for the Prophecy, all hope would be lost. The Prophecy has brought you to us and restored hope for our people. Many have died fulfilling it—among them, Malchior, husband of Mardra and father of Frinz."

Zabrina paused for a moment, in respect for Malchior's memory. "Malchior's life was taken by a Death Spell, the darkest of all magic. Thurnangl forbids mention or thought of the eight great death spells, but they are practiced without disapproval in Garzula's lands.

"Malchior was once thought to be the bearer of the Prophecy, and upon his death, Thurnangl mourned its own destruction. Hope was revived at the birth of Frinz, and though Sürnam's army gained in victory, hope lingered in Thurnangl's leaders. Fearing for her daughter's safety, Mardra hid Frinz from the world, and Thurnangl became a land of despair."

At this, Crystal interrupted, "Why wasn't Frinz shown to the people of Thurnangl? Shouldn't they be given hope?"

"Ahhh, my child," Zabrina continued, "if the people of Thurnangl had known of Frinz, then so too would Sürnam. He would have stopped at nothing to destroy her, and the Prophecy, for good. Sacrifices were made so that the Prophecy might save us all."

Crystal looked away in embarrassment and fear.

"But, fear not," Zabrina soothed, "Those rules were put into place while Frinz grew. We knew it would not last forever. You are safe here. There is nothing to fear when you are here under our protection."

Zabrina paused for a moment, considering the words that would best explain. "For all that lose hope, there are those who gain it. Many people threw aside the Prophecy as an untrue tale, but still the people fight for a better world. They fight for their families and their futures, prophecy or no."

"But why exactly do Sürnam's people attack? They can't simply be jealous?" Brant asked.

The faces around the table displayed an array of emotions as all considered Brant's questions.

Finally, after a moment of silence, Zabrina spoke, "But such is true. Nothing drives their evil desire to conquer more than their greed. As I said before, they seek to destroy the power they cannot possess. The

Stone has not chosen them for great magic, and thus they must destroy it. None in Garzula know of its location. Very few from Thurnangl have this knowledge, among them yourselves, Frinz, Mardra, Liane, Raymond, Arron, and myself." Crystal alone noted the pink that blossomed across Frinz's cheeks as Zabrina spoke the last name.

Zabrina continued, "But the people of Garzula do not know the Stone's true purpose. It serves as more than a source of powerful magic. It is our life source. To destroy it would be to destroy this world."

At her words, the orb overhead displayed a decimated landscape with a lone figure standing in its midst. He had blond hair, almost white in its fairness, which hung to his shoulders. He stared into the distance, his face expressionless except for the hatred in his black eyes. This embodiment of evil could only be Sürnam. Crystal gasped involuntarily as the screen blackened and all fell silent. Zabrina waited for the group to recover from the sight of Sürnam before concluding her explanation.

"When the stone has been made safe and Sürnam defeated, we shall erase Death Spells from Thurnangl so that they may no longer harm our people. Sürnam holds another weapon which is unmatched by any in our land—the ability to teleport. He created a spell known only to himself and his assistant, Aaliyah, and can use it to travel magically from one place to another. He is, however, limited in his travels to places he has been. He can only transport short distances, while Frinz alone can go as far as she wishes. Teleporting is severely limited and requires much strength, but all magic comes with a price. Sürnam's spells are deadly and dangerous, and dark magic blackens his heart and those of his followers. They can be stopped; They must be stopped."

In silence, the group cleared the table and prepared to retire for the evening. Wrought from their long day and the tale they had just heard, Crystal and Brant bid their hosts goodnight and made their way to bed. Crystal's sleep was immediate and troubled, but Brant lay awake for many hours, haunted by Sürnam's face. His last thought as he met with sleep was of the danger that awaited them. Sürnam was out there, and he wanted them dead.

CHAPTER 9

COMING DANGER, HIDDEN LOVE

The large, black bird made its way through the night skies over the land of Garzula. It flew with unnatural speed, soaring over the camps of Sörnam's armies, its form invisible in the dark night. It flew over the castle gates of Phärnam, bobbing and weaving past all manner of dark creature, as it made its way to Sörnam's throne room. Hopping from the sill, it transformed from bird to man and approached swiftly, bowing before Sörnam.

"Have you worthy news for me this time, Caddock?" Sörnam asked coldly.

Caddock stepped back, stung by Sörnam's iciness. Recovering, he smiled wickedly as he said, "Master, I do believe you will find my news especially interesting today." Caddock's dead, dark eyes—the mark of Sörnam's followers—were half hidden by his stringy, black hair.

At a nod from his master, he continued. "While making my way through the mountains, I happened upon three travelers—a young witch, a boy, and a girl. The witch had hair of the deepest red, and she traveled with a dragon, yet it was her companions who caught my eye. The boy with eyes the color of the forest canopy and hair of brown seemed inseparable from the young maiden whose hair was like spun gold and whose eyes shown like sapphires. I heard the young witch call them by name—Brant and Crystal."

Sörnam's raged boiled over uncontrollably as he leapt from his thrown. "The Prophecy! All these years we though it destroyed! How could we have been wrong? Where are these travelers now?"

Caddock cowered at his master's question, knowing his answer to be insufficient. "I know not, Master. I could follow them no further." Fear shook Caddock, and he shrank from Sörnam's wrath.

"And why not, Caddock?" Sörnam asked, his voice slicing through the tension that permeated the room. "Why, when you could have followed and dispatched them, do you stand before me with this news? Incompetent fool!" Sörnam struck the man cowering at his feet, letting the sound ring through the room. No one spoke.

Composing himself, Caddock risked Sörnam's wrath and spoke his piece. "I tried, Master, but I could not follow. They were protected by an unseen force, a shield that would not let me pass."

Sörnam's response was interrupted by the arrival of a young woman at the throne room door. The guards shrank from her as she passed, and she ignored all before her as she made her way to Sörnam. She marched forward, her indigo hair hanging to her waist. The black pools of her dead eyes were hard and unfeeling. She bowed before Sörnam.

"You have news, Aaliyah?" Sörnam asked, composing himself.

She stared, unblinking. "Yes, Master. One of our spies has sent word from Meclen. The children of the Prophecy—"

"Yes, Yes," Sörnam waved her words away impatiently.

"Caddock was just telling me of their arrival. It seems he has failed to capture them." Sörnam shook his head in mock disappointment, while his eyes conveyed an unspoken threat. "What say you, Aaliyah? Shall we give him one last chance to prove himself?"

Aaliyah fixed Caddock with her dead eyes, studying his face as she considered. "He has let them escape. Should he not, then, find and destroy them?"

Sörnam's mirthless chuckle was more terrifying than his anger. "Quite right, my dear," he said, turning to Caddock. "You will take a band of spies to the mountains and seek out these children of the Prophecy. When you find them, you shall destroy them and all that stand in your way. In one month, we march on Thurnangl and make our way to Keldom. The children must not be alive to stop us. GO!" Sörnam dismissed the sniveling Caddock who, fearing greater punishment, morphed immediately into his bird form and exited in the manner he had entered.

Satisfied, Sörnam turned to Aaliyah. "Don't leave just yet, my pet. I have a very important job for you."

An evil smirk stretched across her lips.

Brant was wide awake, unable to sleep for fear of what nightmares may come. He stared at the flames flickering across the enchanted ceiling, doing his best to banish Sörnam's cold stare from his mind.

"Brant, you're awake?" Crystal asked.

In answer, Brant threw a pillow across the room. Crystal, caught off guard, shrieked and tumbled out of the bed.

"Ouch," she said, her pride hurt as much as her backside.

Seeing her embarrassment, Brant sighed, got out of bed, and extended his hand. "Hey, I'm sorry. Don't be mad. Although you're cute when you pout like that."

Crystal smiled at his words and, blushing, took the hand he offered. *Why am I blushing? It's just Brant!* she thought.

"Let's get a snack," he offered, pulling her to her feet.

Raiding the kitchen, they found leftover muffins and made themselves comfortable by the living room fire.

"Why don't we go practice tomorrow? I have a feeling I could do more with my powers, if only we could practice," Brant said.

Crystal smiled, but her voice held concern. "There is still so much to learn and do, so much to take in. It worries me to think of it all."

"Then don't think about it," Brant answered. "We need to concentrate on the here and now. We have hard work ahead of us, and worry will just distract you. We can't think about failure. Instead, we have to push on and help these people save their world."

Crystal beamed, uplifted by his words. "You're right."

They returned to their room, and Brant fell immediately to sleep. His visions of Sörnam long gone, he dreamed instead of the blue-eyed girl who held his heart.

Crystal found herself unable to sleep, her thoughts swimming with the one fear she could not shake. She looked at Brant, sleeping peacefully, and found herself smiling. *I will not lose him,* she told herself. She fell asleep, comforted by the thought that, together, they could survive anything.

The others were already beginning their day when Crystal made her way downstairs the next morning.

Entering the kitchen, she found Mardra and Brant finishing their breakfast.

"How long did I sleep?" Crystal asked groggily.

"Long enough," he laughed.

"Well why didn't you wake me?" she demanded playfully.

"Didn't feel like it," Brant retorted. He held his composure for only a moment before they burst into fits of laughter.

"It looks like the two of you are very lively in the morning," Mardra said with a chuckle.

Crystal ate, and Brant waited for her. She was about to take her last delicious bite when Brant swiped the fork from her hand and ate it himself.

"HEY! That was mine," she said crossly.

Brant laughed and cleared her plate and fork, placing them in the wash basin.

Shaking her head, Crystal took his hand and led him from the room. Brant blushed as he let her tug him through the kitchen door.

Mardra chuckled to herself as she watched them leave.

They stepped into the beautifully sunlit morning, and Crystal stretched her arms delightedly to the sky. "What a perfect day!"

"It sure is," Brant said, studying her with a smile.

"Didn't Frinz say there was a river nearby? Let's go see if we can find it!" Crystal's excitement was contagious, and soon they were walking through the forest, enjoying the gentle breeze.

They walked casually through the peaceful forest, enjoying the warm air wafting through the trees. Though there was no path, they found the forest easy to navigate and walked along enjoying the animals they met along the way. Crystal laughed as a tiny imp of a creature descended from the treetops onto Brant's head. Chattering away as though the teens understood every word, their new furry friend jumped into Crystal's arms and used its orange paws to stroke her face. Its long tale stood straight from its body, providing balance as it reached up to lick Crystal's nose before scampering away. Crystal giggled in delight as Brant shook his head. On they went, enjoying the beauty of their day.

In a short time, they reached river. Its waters were deep and clear, peppered with fish of all shapes and colors darting to and fro. The sun shone warmly through the tree branches, casting a brilliant glow on the waters below.

Crystal climbed the nearest tree and hung from a branch letting her fingers tickle the water's surface. Brant joined her, manipulating the rock in his hand into various shapes. Crystal gathered water from the river and moved it through the air. She concentrated, freezing it into icicles which thawed and froze again at her bidding.

"Brant!" she said laughing as she brought the frozen water within inches of his face.

Brant cringed, and Crystal's laughter ceased. "Did you really think I would hit you?" she asked, concerned.

"Of course not," he scoffed, dropping the earth he held into the waters below. He drew out a handful of mud. "Hey Crystal!" he shouted.

She looked up as the mud hit her forehead and responded with a huge wave of water, soaking them both.

They heard the branch crack and had no time to think before it broke, plunging them into the river below. They emerged, soaking wet and surprised.

"You should have seen your face!" Brant laughed, collapsing on the riverbank.

Crystal sat beside him and ruffled his wet hair. "I was too busy looking at yours!"

As their gazes locked, the air between them charged with unseen energy. They looked away with red faces.

Crystal pulled the water from her clothes and did the same for Brant. They sat in comfortable silence, practicing their powers and enjoying the beauty of the day.

Brant studied Crystal intently as she played with the water in her hand, forming it into icy crystals, which she dispatched into the surrounding trees. Feeling his gaze upon her, Crystal turned and smiled. Brant returned the smile briefly before turning his attention to the rock in his hand. He weighed it, considering the possibilities, and then concentrated hard on its shape. He used his hands to manipulate the stone, until at last he held what passed as a sword. Brandishing it in the air in front of him, he smiled in satisfaction. It was far from perfect.

But if I ever need to protect her, it will do, he thought.

Crystal called out excitedly, "Brant, look at this!"

He walked toward her and stopped. "You're not going to hit me, right?" he teased.

"Shut up and watch," Crystal said with a wink and stretched her hand to the sky. The tiny crystals shot into the air and exploded, falling around them in glittering sparkles, a truly dazzling scene.

Just then, Crystal noticed that the sun was getting low in the sky. "Have we been out here almost the whole day? No way!" She exclaimed.

"I guess we were having just so much fun that time moved by without us noticing." Brant said, a smile on his lips.

Crystal blushed slightly, and they began the walk back to Frinz's cottage. The house was in sight when Crystal suddenly stopped, glancing at a nearby tree with a smile. She was up the tree before Brant could blink.

"What are you doing?" he asked with a laugh.

"I'm going to watch the sunset," she said without looking down.

She reached the top of the tree after nearly half an hour of climbing. Careful to ensure the branches would hold her wait, Crystal looked up to see the most breathtaking sight since her arrival in Thurnangl. The sun had reached the tree line and was just about to set completely.

Brant joined her on the tree branch and gasped, "Oh wow, this is so cool!"

"Isn't it?" she said, unable to avert her eyes from the beautiful scene.

Brant kept his eyes on Crystal, transfixed. A small smile played on his lips as he studied her. She felt his eyes resting on her, and she tore her eyes from the mesmerizing sunset.

As their eyes met, something changed between them. Both experienced a new feeling in their hearts that could not yet be expressed. Neither spoke, for the moment was too precious. They stayed there, together, drinking in their new reality and relishing its perfection.

The moment was as fleeting as the setting sun, but the new feelings still lingered. Crystal and Brant snapped back to reality and smiled shyly at each other.

"I guess.....I guess we should get back to Frinz and the others," Crystal said, blushing slightly.

"Yeah, I guess they're going to get worried," Brant said.

Carefully, they climbed down the tree and walked back to the house, holding hands and knowing they were closer, somehow.

CHAPTER 10

THE PASSING OF THE SHADOWS

That dinner was a very cheerful one. The change in Brant and Crystal was tangible and a powerful new aura shimmered between them.

Frinz sat, watching the pair, before speaking in hushed tones to her mother. "I have no problem with them loving each other," she said with a small smile. "Liane told me this would happen. Can you feel the power between them? They radiate a force stronger than love and more powerful than any bond I have seen before."

Mardra and Zabrina nodded their agreement.

"This is very good!" Crystal complimented the meal as they were all finishing their last few bites.

"So, did you both have fun today?" Zabrina asked, a hint of mischief in her voice.

Crystal and Brant blushed as one. "Yes, yes we did," they said together.

The evening passed pleasantly, and Brant and Crystal made for bed early, exhausted from their eventful day. The next morning, they were up at dawn and ready for another day of discovery. At breakfast, they told Frinz and Zabrina of their adventures, leaving out their intimate sunset moment. They ate hurriedly and were out the door once more, eager to see what awaited them this day.

"Well this should be interesting," Zabrina laughed with a wink at her friend.

"Yes, my dear friend, it shall be," Frinz said, smiling.

Crystal and Brant laughed as they ran toward the river, stopping short at its banks. They paused, captivated by the beautiful sites surrounding them.

"So what are we——," Brant began but was cut off.

"Wait. Before you say anything, watch this," Crystal said. She balanced on the very edge of the riverbank and placed her hand over the sparkling water below. At the tiniest wave of her hand, the water ceased its movement and stood completely still, frozen by her powers. Admiring her handiwork, Crystal glided onto the ice but immediately fell. Brant giggled as he effortless let himself glide to her side.

"Are you ok?" he asked.

Crystal pouted in reply. "Show off."

"It's ok. Skating isn't that hard. Here, I'll show you." Brant pulled Crystal to her feet and put his arm around her waist. Crystal blushed at his touch.

He took both of her hands and skated in front of her, guiding her across the smooth surface.

"See. You can do it. One-two, one-two."

Crystal concentrated hard, doing her best not to fall again. It took a while, and a few close calls, but Crystal began to improve.

"I'm going to let go, ok?" Brant said, slowly loosening his grip on her hands.

"Oh wait, but I—," Crystal protested. Brant let go, and she was gliding slowly on her own.

"See. It's not so bad," Brant said with a smile.

Gradually, Crystal's confidence improved, as did her skill. She made her way down the frozen river, Brant following close behind.

He could hear her whispering softly "One-two, one-two."

He smiled as they skated together, enjoying the sun shining through the branches of the trees. Though the weather was warm, the ice showed no signs of melting.

They continued on, their skating becoming more fluid and in sync. Brant spun suddenly in front of Crystal, offering his hand with a deep bow. She giggled as she curtsied and placed her hand in his. They dipped and twirled, Brant teaching Crystal the nuances of their dance. It was soon clear that they were no longer alone, for the animals of the forest had come to see the curious sight of the frozen river.

Brant pointed out a large creature with moss-like fur standing before them, testing the ice. It bore antlers larger than those of an elk, and its back glistened with spikes the color of emeralds. Its long tail swished behind it, helping it balance as it stumbled onto the ice.

Brant and Crystal smiled at the strange creature and watched as many others made their way onto the gleaming surface of the frozen river. Crystal resumed skating, as the two continued on in a comfortable silence.

Crystal created a ramp of ice and drew back, preparing to test it. Brant, slow to realize her plan, held out his hand to stop her. Crystal laughed and took a deep breath.

Brant closed his eyes. He couldn't watch.

She skated toward the ramp, moving faster with each step. She glided up its smooth slope, launching herself into midair and landing on the platform that sprung up before her. She bowed, beaming with pride.

Crystal jumped down from her platform and looked back at Brant with a smirk. "Bet you can't catch me!" she cried and skated away as fast as she could.

Brant called after her, "Oh! We'll see about that!"

Crystal noticed that they were venturing a little too far from their starting point, and she turned around, skating right past Brant. He reached out to steady himself and grabbed Crystal's shirt, tumbling them both to the ground.

They landed together, their faces so close they were almost touching. Caught in the moment, they stared at each other, unwilling to move, hearts pounding in unison.

The ice beneath them suddenly turned back to water, and they fell into the river. Rising to the surface, they looked at each and burst into laughter.

"I'm sorry. I lost concentration. I didn't know that would happen," Crystal said apologetically.

"It's not a problem," Brant said truthfully.

They swam to the water's edge, and Brant pulled Crystal from the water. They rested together in a small patch of grass where the sun was shining through the trees.

The cool water felt soothing in the heat of the sun. The two sat in silence, their eyes closed, reveling in the warmth of the day.

Brant spoke quietly, "Hey, Crystal?"

"Hm?"

"You know I'm never going to forget this, right? This is so amazing, making these memories with you. It's... like I can't put it into words. I want them to last forever, and I won't let them go."

"Me neither, Brant. You know we'll always be together." Crystal looked over at Brant, and he returned her gaze.

Brant blushed as he realized how close their faces were. Crystal gave a tender smile, and her eyes glistened in the sunlight. It was the perfect moment. Brant was so close to her now, so close that he could almost—

"What are you two doing?" said a familiar voice.

Crystal and Brant sat up with a start as Frinz came toward them, a knowing smile on her lips. "Come on, you two. Dinner is almost prepared." Frinz beckoned them to follow.

They had whiled away another day in the forest, intent on nothing but each other. They followed in silence, their faces still warm from the heat of their day.

Upon reaching the house, they were met by delicious fragrances coming from the kitchen. The house had been decorated with ribbons, and little bubbles in every color imaginable floated around the room. Soft music wafted through the air.

"What's the occasion?" Brant asked.

"Oh, this is an ancient holiday. Every year, on the fourth full moon, we celebrate the Passing of the Shadows. It is a traditional holiday representing that spring has come, and winter is finally at its end," Mardra explained, placing a tray of freshly baked sweets on the counter. Brant and Crystal, hungry from a day of skating, delved into the delightful treats at once.

"Where is the music coming from?" Crystal asked, her mouth full. She listened in awe to the most beautiful music she had ever heard, a cacophony of sounds weaving stories in the air.

"It comes from our memory. If we have a song that we like and we have heard before, then we can let the song be heard from our thoughts," Frinz explained.

"Wow! That's so cool! I wish I could try it," Crystal said, wishing now that she could use magic.

"I can assist you with that," Frinz said happily. She touched a finger to Crystal's forehead and recited a spell.

The air was filled with the sound of a song unknown to Frinz, Mardra, and Zabrina, but Crystal and Brant knew it all too well. Crystal began to sing, the words and notes long memorized. Her voice carried through the house, its pureness and beauty shocking even Brant. He had not heard Crystal sing in a long time, and the sound touched him, as though his heart were an instrument only she could play. All too soon, the song ended. Crystal looked around, surprised at the awed faces staring back at her.

"I'm sorry. I'm a little out of practice," Crystal apologized, blushing.

"No, on the contrary, it was beautiful. I have never heard any sound like it," Mardra said.

Crystal looked down in embarrassment. "Thank you very much."

Brant looked at her and smiled, "I haven't heard you sing in a long time. It was good to hear your beautiful voice again."

Brant's words made her blush all the more.

For the rest of the evening, they spoke of the Passing of the Shadows traditions—of the parties and festivities that normally accompanied the day. This year, they would celebrate at home, for Brant and Crystal could not be shown to the world. Not yet. Crystal and Brant apologized, but Mardra silenced them with a kind smile. "There is no need to apologize. We are here with family."

Mardra beckoned them outside, and the group gathered under the shining moonlight. The glistening orb grew brighter, and suddenly the forest around them came to life. The trees blossomed with flowers, and the leaves changed to a lush and healthy green. The forest floor, once littered with fallen leaves and branches, became lush with soft grass and moss. A new season dawned, signaling a new beginning for the land. With that, the happy party spent the remainder of their magnificent holiday together, celebrating and reveling in each other's company.

CHAPTER 11

A CAVE OF WONDER

The next morning, Crystal woke before Brant and dressed quickly. She had made a plan for their day and couldn't wait to share it with him. She grabbed her pillow and swatted Brant's sleeping form.

"Come on, sleepy, wake up! We have a big day planned," she said loudly.

Brant buried his face in his pillow and muttered, "Go away. I want to sleep."

Crystal sighed in feigned exasperation. "Well that's fine. I don't mind travelling to the waterfall in the forest alone. Frinz said it could be dangerous, but I'm sure I'll be fine. I'll just have to eat a picnic by the shores of the waterfall's big lake all by myself. I don't mind."

Brant groaned and shook his head. "Fine. I'll go, but only to make sure you don't drown."

"Are you kidding? I'm Crystal, Mistress of Water. How could I drown?"

Only you could find a way, Brant thought.

Crystal squealed in delight before bounding down the stairs. She sprang into the kitchen and shouted, "Good morning!" Her excitement was met with silence. She was the only one stirring in the first light of dawn.

Good, Crystal thought, *it's early yet, and we have the entire day in front of us.*

She was packing the picnic basket when Brant came down the stairs, still rubbing the sleep from his eyes.

He examined her work and chuckled, "Are we really going to have a picnic?"

"Of course! Frinz said the view was just gorgeous and the water is crisp and cool. It'll be so much fun!" Crystal grinned with anticipation.

Crystal finished her preparations by leaving a note for Mardra and the others. No sense in worrying their hosts with their absence.

They walked toward the river, enjoying the early morning sunshine through the trees. Crystal carried the picnic basket while Brant studied the map in confusion.

"Where is this waterfall? I don't see it on the map."

She leaned in closely to look over Brant's shoulder. He blushed slightly. "It's right here, silly, just downstream. We'll be there in no time!" Crystal skipped away.

Brant sighed and followed.

They continued through the forest, eager to reach their destination. The sound of rushing water grew louder as they turned the final bend.

"The waterfall!" Crystal and Brant exclaimed together.

They ran faster, and when they came to the area where the trees cleared, they saw a breathtaking scene. The water was pure and clear, and the lake was much bigger than they had imagined. It sparkled with the sun's rays. Ripples form the waterfall danced across its surface as animals at the lake's edge drank peacefully from the pristine water.

"Wow, this is so beautiful! Thurnangl never seems to bore me." Crystal said, gazing across the vast lake that spread before them. She looked over the river to see rocks jutting out above the water's surface in a line that would be easy to walk. She set down the picnic basket and skipped nimbly across the rocks.

"What are you doing?! You're going to fall!" Brant shouted over the roar of the falls.

"Wow! Brant, look at this! The waterfall is so high!" Crystal said looking down at the water below.

Brant inched nearer to her. "If you fall, I'm never going forgive you."

"It's ok. I won't," Crystal said reassuringly.

"Wow! You're right. This view is amazing!" Brant said.

Just as he finished his sentence, an enormous fish, the size of a small car, jumped from the river behind them. They turned in unison as it leapt over them. Its tail slapped Crystal in the face as it dove into the lake below, and she began to fall backward over the falls. Brant reached out to grab her hand, brushing her fingers tips, but he was too late. She fell over the waterfall, her screams lost in the roar of rushing water.

"CRYSTAL!" Brant yelled as he watched her fall to the lake below.

With a swish of his hand he fashioned stairs in the side of the cliff that they led to the lake's edge. He grabbed the picnic basket and ran, his eyes never leaving the water's surface.

Crystal had not emerged. Brant's heart raced faster.

Crystal felt herself touch the bottom of the lake and opened her eyes. She looked up to see the surface, barely visible above. She kicked off from the bottom of the lake, her lungs aching for air. When at last she could take no more, she acted instinctively. Cupping her hands in front of her face, she created an air bubble around her mouth and nose using the air captured in the water by tiny bubbles. She smiled in delight and surveyed the waters around her. Fish of every size and color swam about. Below her, she saw a furry purple-coated creature making its way through the water, its four legs paddling hard. Its long tail fin twitched as it eyed her, before swimming off in the other direction.

Crystal looked up at the surface, not too far away now, and she could see Brant standing at the water's edge. He looked frantically from side to side, still searching for her. Crystal swam to the edge of the lake, just out of his eyesight, and burst from the water. Grabbing his hand, she pulled him in.

Crystal?! He thought.

Brant's shock at her appearance left him breathless, and he turned toward the surface, in need of air. Crystal grabbed his shirt, and he looked at her in panic. She smiled and cupped her hands in front of his mouth. A pocket of air formed, and Brant found he could breathe easily. He looked at her in astonishment.

Crystal smiled. "You see, we can breathe with the bubbles of air I created." Her voice was only slightly muffled by the air bubble, and she beckoned him down into the water's depths. "Come on! Let's explore!"

Brant stopped, staring at Crystal. "Why didn't you come up earlier? I thought you had drowned."

She paused, looking away for a moment. "I'm sorry, Brant. I didn't know that I could breathe underwater or make it so that others could. I was having fun. I didn't think of how I must have worried you. I'm sorry," she apologized, taking his hand. "Come on! Let's swim together."

Brant sighed, "Why not?"

They swam on, delighted in their underwater playground, giving names to every creature they found. As they swam, they were amazed at the many animals they met. Fish and other water creatures swam about them, a whirl of color in the sparkling water.

The sun shone down from the surface above, reflecting and refracting the gorgeous colors of the lake's inhabitants. Their fish friends departed suddenly, and Crystal looked around, feeling uneasy. A snarl from the depths made them change course quickly. A fur-coated animal with clawed fins and snarling teeth barreled towards them. Fearing they could not outswim the unknown assailant, Crystal created a current and, holding Brant's hand tightly, rode it to the waterfall.

They swam under the waterfall's roaring waters and emerged in a cave. Spotting dry ground, they scrambled onto the cave floor, and stared around with wide eyes. The cave was entirely lined with sparkling gemstones and cast a brilliant glow on Crystal and Brant. The light danced across the cave floor. They stood, completely dazzled.

They heard the snarl again, this time behind them. Turning, they spotted the creature glaring at them from just beneath the water's surface, its red eyes hungry and menacing.

Crystal yelped with fright and clung to Brant. He put his arms around her and laughed.

"It's ok. I don't think it can come up onto dry land," Brant said.

"Oh, I see," Crystal stammered, embarrassed. She realized she was in Brant's arms, and she blushed as her heart beat faster. She could feel Brant's uneven heartbeat as well. She looked into his eyes, sparkling with the light of the cave crystals.

They leaned in closer until there was little room between them. An inch closer still, and—

The creature, glaring balefully at them from the water, gave a piercing cry that shook the cave.

Crystal turned, infuriated by the ruined moment. "ENOUGH!!!" she yelled and froze the creature in ice.

"Wow, I didn't know you got angry so easily," Brant teased.

Crystal didn't say anything for some time. She had her back turned to Brant, tears of frustration glistening in her eyes. She then sighed realizing that the moment was ruined and that she was hungry.

She smiled at Brant. "Let's have lunch!"

"Ok," he agreed.

They jumped into the water and swam out of the cave. Their frozen enemy was nowhere to be seen, having sunk with the weight of the ice. Brant sighed, disappointed at the creature's interruption. He was sure they would have their moment—someday.

Emerging from the lake, Crystal and Brant went to the spot where he had left the picnic basket. They lay down on the warm grass looking up at the trees.

"Well, that was sure fun, huh?" Brant said, turning to his side and looking at Crystal.

"Yeah it was! The little animals here are so cute!"

They pulled out the blanket from the picnic basket and arranged it on the ground. Crystal pulled the water from their cloths, and they both fell back onto the blanket eating their lunch.

As they ate, they made up names for the strange animals they'd seen during their swim. Pillermids were the perfect name for the purple friend who had followed them through the water, and Crystal knew that the tiny colorful fish which swam in large schools were to be called dotfish, the same fish that swam in her room at the cottage. Crystal and Brant spent their meal happily devising names for creatures big and small and laughing all the while.

Not long after they were done eating, Crystal closed her eyes. Brant's voice lulled her to sleep.

"Don't you think so, Crystal? Crystal?" Brant looked over at Crystal to see her fast asleep.

He smiled, leaned over, and kissed her on the forehead.

Close enough, he though, *for now.*

Brant settled in beside Crystal, soothed by the warm breeze and shining sun into a peaceful sleep.

It was a long time before Crystal woke up. She sat up and rubbed her eyes.

"I fell asleep?" she said, looking around. She noticed that it was dark, too dark.

She shook Brant awake. "Brant! Brant! Wake up!"

"Huh? What do you want? I was—," Brant cut himself off, sitting straight up. He looked around too and noticed it had grown late. "We should get moving. I don't like the woods too much after dark."

They gathered their things and made for the cliff wall.

"How are we going to get back up? I thought you climbed down," Crystal said, unable to see the rock wall in the darkness.

"We'll just take the rock stairs, made by yours truly." Brant grinned in satisfaction.

Through the dark, he could see the worry on her face and took her hand. "Don't worry. I won't let you slip through my fingers again." They looked at each other and blushed. Crystal nodded, and they started up the rock steps.

They reached the top of the steps and rushed to make their way home. When the house was finally in view, they could see Frinz pacing outside. She saw them running and her relief turned to anger.

"Where in the world have you two been?! Do you have any idea how late it is?! We were so worried! We though you to be lost! Do you know how—,"

Mardra put a hand on Frinz's shoulder.

"There is no need to be angry, my child. You see? Their faces show their remorse. Yelling will solve nothing. Let us only be thankful that they return unharmed."

Frinz sighed, "Why did you stay out so late? What in the world were you doing?"

Crystal and Brant glanced at one another and laughed sheepishly.

"We sort of fell asleep by the lake. We really had no idea it was so late. We didn't mean to worry you. Sorry," Crystal said apologetically.

"You should both go inside now, before I turn you into fish," Frinz said softly.

Crystal and Brant ran straight upstairs.

Frinz shook her head and returned to the house. "Mother, I fear this adventure will be a long and tasking one for all of us. Those two think little of the dangers around them, so lost are they in their play."

Mardra laughed. "They remind me of what it was like to have you as a young woman."

Frinz gave her mother a hard look and retired for the evening.

"Children. They are all the same, are they not?" Zabrina asked when Frinz had departed.

"Yes, it seems that way. And yet, they fill us with joy and happiness unlike anything in this world."

Zabrina smiled. "You are such a very kind mother, Mardra."

"I do love to think so," Mardra replied, beaming.

In their room, Brant and Crystal laughed as they threw pillows at each other. Feathers flew about the room, and the Children of the Prophecy were, for a time, only children.

Chapter 12
A Call to Battle

"You asinine fool!!" Sörnam shouted as he lashed out at Caddock.

Caddock's mission into the mountains had met with failure. His warriors could not break through Malchior's shield.

"I tried, Master. I—we truly did. We d-did all that we could! We used all the p-power we could muster," Caddock wept.

"I care little for your wasted efforts!" Sörnam roared, his wrath piercing the armor of even his bravest guards. Turning to Caddock, he spoke softly, the icy calm of his words more terrifying than his shouts. "We will deal with this later. For now, a more important matter is at hand." Sörnam turned to walk away.

"Oh thank you, Master, thank you. I will try—," Caddock's words stopped Sörnam dead in his tracks. Turning, he made his way back to the worm of a man.

Sörnam spoke quietly, the ice in his voice chilling his minion to the core. "Try? We do not try, my sniveling underling. We succeed. But," a sinister laugh escaped his lips, "you need not trouble yourself. Your pitiful efforts are no longer required." Sörnam spread a hand in front of Caddock's eyes.

"No Master. Please, I beg you. Please," Caddock cried desperately.

Sürnam ignored the cowering man's plea. "Amzelo," he said softly.

The death spell took hold, and Caddock fell back, a look of terror etched permanently on his face. After a few agonizing moments, his lifeless body sagged to the floor.

Aaliyah made her way into the throne room, her eyes empty and unblinking as she approached her master. Reaching Caddock's lifeless corpse, she stepped over him gracefully, as if stepping over a sleeping dog, and bowed before the throne. Her purple hair flowed like silk over her shoulders to her waist.

"What you have asked of me is done. The Mentordor have come with me, Master. They arrive in great numbers and await your command." Aaliyah spoke in a voice void of emotion.

"Good," Sürnam said, his voice slicing through the air. A nearby guard flinched and prayed that his weakness went unnoticed. "The Mentordor will be a great help. We will see how well the children fight in battle." He let out an icy laugh of satisfaction.

A young woman hid in the shadows, listening with a heavy heart. She would not let his evil spread. She was Sürnam's greatest weakness, the one who knew him best—Lilly.

More than a month had come and gone in Thurnangl, and Crystal and Brant marveled at all they had learned. They had mastered control of earth and water and were compelled by unseen forces to begin new work—Crystal with air and Brant with fire.

Liane came to visit and was delighted at their progress. They handled water and earth with surprising ease. Crystal was able to demonstrate the art of healing, which she had been working closely with Zabrina to perfect. She was just beginning to successfully heal broken bones and deep wounds.

Having no one to help him with his fencing outside of the simple moves Frinz had taught him, Brant was at a loss. He simply focused on his earth and fire work. Frinz assured Brant that he would master his ability soon and gave him books of instruction and technique. Brant found the notes scribbled in the margins most helpful in refining his basic skill. Liane had noticed the difference in the connection between Crystal and Brant.

To Frinz, Liane said only, "We knew this would happen, and we must be glad. Love can only make them stronger as they face what is to come."

Liane soon departed, and the group's attention returned to learning and laughing together in the hidden cottage. Days passed, and Brant and Crystal were becoming comfortable with their new elemental powers, little by little.

On a beautiful morning, as Mardra prepared breakfast and the others rested by the fire, Zabrina sat up suddenly. "Someone is at the door," she said with a smile at Frinz.

"We'll get it!" Brant and Crystal said in unison, rushing for the door.

Brant reached the entrance first and opened the door to a handsome young man. He stood tall and regal in a coat of gleaming armor. The sandy hair upon his head perfectly framed eyes of rich orange. Behind him stood a towering four-legged animal with a flowing, golden mane. The stunning scales on its body shimmered and reflected the colors from the surrounding forest. The creature had three long horns on the top of its head and a long, regal neck. The heavily-armored saddle on its back signified its position as steed to the man before them. The handsome young man smiled and bowed, his helmet grasped in his hands.

"Hello, Crystal and Brant, it is indeed a great honor to meet you."

Crystal and Brant were quickly learning the customs and mannerisms of Thurnangl and returned the bow in kind.

"Please forgive me," said the stranger. "I am one of the few people who know of this cottage. I am a great friend of Frinz," he continued, beaming at the mention of their fair friend. "My name is Arron, Master of the Blades."

"Arron! Frinz has told us about your great adventures. Please come in," Crystal said, ushering him in.

Leading his steed by its reigns, Arron stepped through the expanding entryway.

Crystal could not help but admire the magnificent creature. "May I ask the name of your friend?"

"Of course, and you may ask any questions that come to mind," Arron answered, patting her head.

At the sight of Brant's steely gaze, Arron quickly withdrew his hand and continued, "My faithful hontros is named Ross. He was a gift from my mother when I was nine, before she passed away. He has been with me through my many travels."

Arron gently stroked Ross's muzzle and whispered, "Stay here."

Dropping the reins, Arron proceeded into the kitchen, followed closely by Crystal and Brant.

As Arron entered the room, Frinz looked up and gasped. Her eyes lit with pleasure as she ran to Arron and wrapped her arms around his neck. "It has been so long. It is good to see you once more," she said.

Arron smiled as he held her close. "I have missed you as well."

"What brings you here after so long?" Frinz asked, stepping back. Noticing his full armor, her face fell. "Really?" Her eyes pleaded with him to dispel her fears.

Arron looked away before answering, "Yes, it came unexpectedly. The battle is mere days away, now. I was sent to retrieve you and the Children of the Prophecy. I am truly sorry."

The group stared at Frinz and Arron.

"I did not expect this to come so quickly," Frinz whispered, fretting with her hair. "How many?" She hoped desperately for a positive answer.

"Thousands," Arron answered. "And the Mentordor are among them."

"This cannot be," Frinz moaned, burying her head in her hands.

"Is there any good news?" Crystal asked hopefully. She wasn't ready for a battle.

"Thankfully, yes," Arron said. "Sörnam and his dragons are not among the army moving on Keldom. He must believe Keldom to be an easy victory, but he is sadly mistaken. Raymond has trained our people well, and we will take Sörnam's forces by surprise."

The fear in the faces around him diminished slightly as Arron continued.

"Raymond awaits the arrival of the Children of the Prophecy before finalizing his plan of attack. We must move quickly and join our brother warriors. Crystal, Brant, I know you are but little trained for a battle such as this, but you are the beacon of hope our people need. We value your presence, your leadership, and your magic. Come, we must hurry."

The small party packed quickly, eager to join Raymond in Keldom. Set with provisions, clothing, and their necessary weapons, they embraced Mardra fiercely before Crystal and Brant climbed onto Zabrina's back. Frinz followed with Arron, and the group was soon waving at Mardra as they descended into the air. Brant felt the warmth of Crystal's hand in his, and their eyes met. They were unsure of what waited for them in Keldom, but there was no turning.

CHAPTER 13
BLEEDING SUNSET

Zabrina, carrying Crystal and Brant, reached the city of Keldom the next day. Frinz and Arron travelled close behind on Ross, the midday sun beating down upon them. When they had rested briefly from their travels, Arron led them toward the outskirts of the city. Travelling the city streets, they were bombarded by the sights and sounds of an army preparing for battle. Men and women passed them, clad in full battle armor, and magic flew about them as warriors honed their skills.

Arron walked along, pointing out persons of great power and describing the abilities that made them invaluable to Raymond's army. "The people who fight are those who possess strength and powerful gifts. We are small next to Sürnam's great army, but we pray that our unique powers and surety of purpose will win the day."

Brant shifted uneasily as he weighed the power of special magic against the might of a vast army. A murmur rippled through the crowd, and Crystal and Brant noticed they were being watched closely. The sight of the Children of the Prophecy was made more impressive by their dragon companion. The group made its way through the throngs, acknowledging their brothers at arms with grace and pride.

The camp of Raymond's army lay on the very outskirts of Keldom, a vast patchwork of tents and practice areas amid the blossoms of the surrounding fields. The air was charged with an anxious anticipation that struck Crystal's very core. She looked down to find her hands shaking. Noticing her tremble, Brant gathered Crystal close.

"We're going to be just fine," he said to her reassuringly.

Crystal shook her head. "I just don't feel like I can do this!" she cried. Looking into his eyes, she saw the same, unspoken fear.

Brant smiled and said, "It's going to be ok, I promise. We don't really have a choice, do we?"

Crystal nodded, and they continued to follow Arron. The group its way through the sea of tents, and soon they arrived at the center of the field. Before them stood a very plain tent, very similar to those surrounding it.

Arron stepped closer to the entrance and ordered, "Wait here for a moment."

The group waited outside the tent, each lost in thought. Crystal fiddled nervously with the locket at her neck, as Brant played with a small flame in his hand.

After a long while, Arron returned and beckoned to them. "My father, Raymond, Leader of the Army, will see you now."

They followed Arron into the tent and were met with an astonishing sight. The space was clearly enchanted to accommodate many people. In the middle of the room sat a large table upon which lay a map of Thurnangl. Witches and wizards huddled around the table, pointing to the map and arguing in hushed tones.

At their entrance, Raymond looked up and smiled. He was a tall man, dressed in armor that bore a golden R on the left shoulder. His eyes, the color of the richest sunset, were offset by his sandy, greying hair. His face told the story of battles won and lost in his years as leader.

"Welcome, Crystal and Brant. I am glad for your safe arrival. Come, we have much to discuss." Raymond motioned them forward. "Before we continue, I would like to introduce you to all who have gathered here at this council—Badrani, Hayachith, Yvett, Saxton and Melvin."

Crystal and Brant nodded to each council member in turn. Badrani was rather old but in no way feeble. He had grey hair and reddish brown eyes that held a stern but kind look.

Hayacinth was young and beautiful, with golden hair that cascaded to her torso. Crystal gazed with envy at the beautiful tresses. The witch's eyes were as white as snow and sparkled as she bowed to them.

Yvett was a proud-looking individual with hair of indigo and eyes the color of a tropical sea. She appeared stern and unwelcoming but smiled as she was introduced.

Saxton, the youngest of the party, was a plain young man in his early twenties. His energetic smile offset the dull green eyes and nondescript hair, bringing a subtle charm to his forgettable visage.

A sensible looking man named Melvin bowed pleasantly, his spectacles sliding from his nose. His ginger hair, smoothed neatly against his brow, brought out the richness of his brown eyes.

The council bowed to Crystal and Brant, who returned the mark of respect.

"I have called this council," Raymond said, "so that we may devise our plan of action."

"But why were we forced to wait until the children arrived?!" Yvett said hotly.

"Because, Yvett," Raymond answered with measured patience, "These are not mere children. They are a necessary part of our victory."

He turned to address Crystal and Brant. "Sürnam's army marches here as we speak. I have heard from our scouts that they will arrive by late morning a day from tomorrow. The number is beyond anything we could have imagined. With them, they bring the Mentordor."

"Mentordor?" Crystal asked.

"The Mentordor," Hyacinth explained, "are a dangerous tribe of beasts, long forgotten. They are said to have lived in these lands long ago, before their souls were blackened by a strange sickness. It poisoned their minds, morphed their very being, and reduced them to monstrous creatures bent on death and destruction. That same strange sickness reduced this land to waste and forced the members of their tribe who were not afflicted to retreat into the safety of the forest. Changed forever, the ill were driven from the land to a hidden valley, where they could no longer harm others. There, they rotted and raged, until their humanity vanished completely. Sürnam found them, and has tamed them to his own purposes."

There was a moment of silence before Brant asked, "What do you think we should do?"

Raymond pointed to the map, indicating a river not far from the city.

"We hope to send a small party to hold Sürnam's forces at the Red River until reinforcements from Fotmáre arrive. We must hope they succeed."

Melvin was next to speak. "We must fight, and fight well. We will have no shelter of tree nor mountain, only the flat land for miles around."

"That can be changed," Brant said. All eyes turned to him.

"Do you mean to say that *you* can change it?" Yvett asked skeptically.

"Yes," Brant replied, his confidence growing, "As a matter of fact, I can."

Brant picked up three stones from the floor and threw them into the air. At his command, the pebbles danced through the air, landing gracefully on the map. Brant smiled, as his audience gasped at the sight. "It would be difficult, but I can give us shelter."

The room was silent as the council studied their guests with unconcealed awe.

Taking her cue from Brant, Crystal stepped forward and spoke bravely. "We are young and inexperienced in battle, but we are the Children of the Prophecy, sent here and granted powers to help in this fight. We are ready. That's why I'll be with the first group to meet the enemy at Red River."

The room erupted in protest.

"But-but you can do no such thing! It is a suicide mission, led by those brave and selfless enough to volunteer their lives," Saxton said, slamming his fist on the table.

"And why not?" Crystal replied. "I will not sit here waiting for backup while the men and women I have sworn to protect risk their lives!"

Crystal squared her shoulders as realization struck her. This was no longer a game. This was war. Brant blinked, awed at Crystal's transformation.

"This is mad!" Badrani shouted. "You are here as a beacon of hope—to be protected, not to meet your death!"

Crystal's words were measured and sure, "If I die here, then so be it. I am charged with protecting these people. You think that Brant and I cannot protect ourselves because we are young? We are the Children of the Prophecy, and we know what awaits us. We will help you win this war or die trying."

The room was silent once more, as the council stared at Crystal in disbelief.

Crystal continued stubbornly, "I will go to the Red River. I will fight to the death if need be, and there is nothing that will change my mind."

Brant could only laugh as he took her hand. "Ladies and gentlemen, you'll find that Crystal rarely changes her mind. She's a stubborn one, and she will see this through."

"Yes," Raymond acquiesced, "we will listen. We cannot ask so much from you and yet keep you away from your purpose. You will meet the party travelling to the Red River at the edge of town. They depart on the morrow at sunset. May your courage and power protect you. This council is adjourned."

Giving a stiff bow, Crystal left the tent, and Brant followed close behind.

When they were removed from the earshot of their companions, Brant turned on Crystal in anger. "What the hell was that?! You aren't in this alone, you know! We're in this together, Crystal!" His shouts drew stares and whispers from onlookers, too intrigued to hide their curiosity.

"Well what do you expect me to do?! Just sit here! Why are you even arguing? You know you can't change my mind." Crystal sighed and took Brant's face in her hands. "Besides, you said we would be just fine, right? Now it's your turn to trust me."

Brant's anger dissipated and was replaced by a different fire as they moved closer together. Taking her chin in his hands, he whispered gently, "I didn't say I was going to stop you, but don't think you're having all of the fun without me."

The moment was broken by Zabrina. "My, you two seemed lively in there," the dragon said, leaning close.

The pair jumped apart, their embarrassment muffling any reply.

Zabrina laughed heartily.

Frinz and Arron emerged from the tent to witness the awkward display before them. Frinz looked to Zabrina for answers, but the dragon only shook her head and smiled.

Frinz turned to Crystal and Brant and spoke solemnly. "Zabrina and I will remain in camp to help the others, while you journey to Red River. We must part to make our preparations. Will you two be alright?"

"Yeah," Crystal said in a small voice.

"We'll be fine," Brant muttered.

Crystal and Brant stood in silence, watching their friends depart.

"Why don't we go see how we can help?" Crystal said, growing excited.

"What are you talking about?" Brant shot her a sideways glance.

"I mean, let's go see what kind of weapons and armor we can make for everyone! Come on! I know just where to go!" Crystal took Brant's hand and ran toward the city.

It did not take long for Crystal and Brant to find the blacksmith. The small shop was working at full steam, and smoke billowed from the windows. Crystal and Brant walked into the scorching room, and saw a muscular man shaping a piece of metal set atop an anvil. His hammer whooshed through the air rhythmically, striking the metal and bending it to his will.

"Excuse me," Crystal said.

The man turned and said heatedly, "Your needs will have to wait, young ones. I am tasked with supplying an army with weapons and armor. An Army! Where these people think I will find the resources or help is beyond me. Even my forging ability, granted by the Stone of Power, cannot bring forth a miracle!"

"That's why we're here," Crystal said kindly. "We thought you might need some help."

The blacksmith stopped, seeing them properly for the first time. He bowed hastily and said, "My humblest apology. My eyes are tired from the work, and I did not recognize you, Crystal and Brant of the Prophecy. I am Rainer, Creator of the Blades."

"You made all of the armor we have seen? That's amazing! It looks so light," Crystal exclaimed.

Rainer beamed at her praise. "Yes I did. The Stone of Power gave me the ability to create magnificent armor that is light and strong. It protects the wearer from sun and storm, its magic shielding men from the elements while they fight. Pardon me, but how do you two plan to craft weapons for an entire army in so little time?"

"Well," Brant said, "leave that to us. We will step outside and begin."

Rainer humbly thanked them and resumed his work.

Once outside, they noticed a line forming in front of the smithy. Crystal and Brant looked at each other and nodded.

Brant gathered a bit of earth and shaped it to form a proper sword. Spinning it in a funnel of fire, he fashioned and forged a weapon of superior quality. He continued on, crafting and stacking swords, as those waiting for weapons and armor stared awe.

Noticing their gazes, Brant smiled and waved a hand in invitation. "Please, take what you need for battle."

Crystal fashioned shields by pulling water deep from under the earth, creating un-melting ice as thick and strong as steel. Soldiers came eagerly forward to test the weapons. Everyone was pleased with their work and happy to be properly equipped for battle. They worked long into the day and were surprised when shadows began to grow long around them.

Brant wiped the sweat from his brow. "I suppose we should find a place to rest for the night."

"I have already arranged it." said Frinz, approaching with a tired smile.

Crystal stretched her tired muscles. "Which tent is it, then?"

Frinz chuckled, "Oh no, the innkeeper graciously offered us a room for the night. Though she protested, she finally accepted my payment for her services. Come, I will show you."

The four heroes walked slowly, talking of the day's accomplishments. Frinz and Zabrina had worked with Raymond and Arron to prepare tactics and strategies of war. When they reached the inn, Zabrina departed to seek a soft spot nearby where she could slumber undisturbed. The trio was welcomed at the door by a plump, elderly woman who bowed graciously.

"I am honored to offer you a room for the night. I know well how a proper rest can strengthen a soldier before battle."

They returned her bow.

"We are grateful to be granted such kindness and hospitality." Frinz replied.

They were shown to their room. The inn was quiet, filled with men and women weary from the preparations of war. It was a simple room, but they welcomed the soft beds awaiting them.

Crystal flopped down on a bed and sighed, "Nothing like home, but man does this feel amazing after a long day."

Frinz smiled, hanging her cloak at the end of the bed. "What will the two of you do tomorrow? It seems that you have already helped so many today."

Brant and Crystal looked at one another, thinking of the day to come. Frinz fell asleep quickly and quietly. Crystal and Brant lay awake long into the night, wondering what the battle ahead would bring. Soon, their bodies succumbed to exhaustion, and they fell into a restless sleep.

Frinz awakened just as the sun broke over the horizon. She smiled at the two young ones sleeping quietly. Her heart ached with worry. She had grown to love her charges far more than she could have ever dreamed. Her eyes brimmed with tears at the thought of losing them to this terrible war. She dried them quickly. *They have been taught well and are far stronger than even I give them credit for.*

Frinz stroked Crystal's rumpled blond hair. "The sun is awake, and so too should be the heroes of Thurnangl. The day before battle is far too important to spend slumbering in bed."

Crystal groaned and turned into her pillow, "I don't want to."

Frinz chuckled. "No one enjoys an early morning, but you will feel better once you are awake and ready for the day."

Brant rubbed his eyes, "It's ok. She's not much for mornings."

The three dressed quietly and walked downstairs, where the innkeeper greeted them cheerfully.

"I expect you slept well?" she asked, bringing food to the soldiers already waiting at tables for breakfast.

"Very well, thank you," Frinz replied, sitting at a nearby table.

Brant and Crystal's took in the sights and sounds of the room, piecing together a picture of preparation for battle. The inn keeper set plates of food before them. Breakfast was bland and simple fare, nothing fancy, but nourishing, nonetheless. Frinz ate without hesitation, knowing her body needed food to carry her through such a day. She noticed Brant and Crystal staring blankly at their plates, lost in thought.

Frinz pulled them into an embrace, "May your troubled souls be stilled and the light guide you. My two dearest ones, you must eat. Your strength depends upon it."

Crystal and Brant smiled and set to their task, eating quickly once they began. When they had finished, they thanked the innkeeper once more and departed for the day.

Frinz turned to leave them. "I shall see if Arron needs assistance. Do you two have a task for today?"

Crystal spoke first, "I'm going to practice healing. I know that I could use some more guidance and practice, especially for tomorrow."

Brant sighed, "I'm going to see if I can find a swordsman, as silly as that sounds. I know I need more training. I just don't know who to ask…"

"A swordsman?" asked a familiar voice behind them.

Brant turned to see Arron, clad in armor, "You say you need a swordsman? Who better to help than Arron, Master of the Blades, the very one who taught Frinz and gave her the books which you now study?"

Brant's looked at the ground sheepishly. "I thought you would be too busy to teach me on a day like today."

Arron threw his head back with a raucous laugh. "My dear boy, I can certainly make time to teach you. You must never be afraid to ask your friends for help when you need it. Now, we should find you a sword to—"

Arron stopped in mid-sentence as he watched Brant levitate a clump of dirt from the ground and hone it into the shape of a sword. With a snap of his fingers, the sword spun around in a wheel of flame. Brant grasped the newly-fashioned sword as the flames subsided. The flawless blade shimmered in his hand.

Arron smiled his approval. "Incredible! Let us hope your skill to wield the blade matches your skill at crafting one."

As the two began to spar, Crystal watched with a grin. Brant fought hard and listened intently to Arron's instructions. His determination ignited Crystal's resolve. She wanted to sharpen her skills as well.

Crystal glanced at Zabrina, who sat watching nearby, "Can we practice as well, Zabrina?"

"Of course my dear," Zabrina replied with a tender smile.

The two walked to a quiet location. Crystal fiddled with the locket around her neck as her eyes started blankly at the ground.

"What troubles you?" Zabrina's voice snapped her back to reality.

"Oh just… Nervous." Crystal said with a forced smile.

Zabrina nudged her gently, "You will be a wondrous champion my dear. I know it. Now," Zabrina knelt down and ignited a flame on top of a small flower. The flames consumed the petals, leaving the core scorched and smoldering.

"Do what you can." Zabrina instructed, stepping aside.

Crystal knelt next to the tiny flower and cupped its charred remains in her palm. She inhaled deeply felt her hands tremble. Clasping her fingers to steady herself, Crystal bowed her head. She feared that, at any moment, her resolve might crumble.

Zabrina's heart ached to see such a happy young soul gripped with the fear of war. Before Zabrina could speak, a short witch with a long purple cloak approached and took Crystal's hands.

"Having trouble, my dear?" she asked with a tender smile.

Crystal could only blink as she tried to find the words. The young witch chuckled. "My name is Wipplebea, Healer of Hearts."

Wipplebea placed her large staff on the ground, tucked a loose strand of burnt umber hair behind her ear, and swept her hands over the flower. The plant sprung to life, its burns completely healed, and petals began to sprout once more.

"If your heart and mind are in alignment, your healing will follow suit. Concentrate on your purpose, and many lives will be saved by your gentle hands. The love and determination manifested in such healing powers will change the fate of this world for the better. Find power and strength in your gift, young one." Wipplebea spoke as though they were lifelong friends. Her bright green eyes sparkled with passion and kinship.

Crystal wiped a tear from her eye and beamed, "Thank you, ma'am. I appreciate your words. I'll do my best!"

Crystal and Brant worked tirelessly throughout the day. They wanted their skills and knowledge sharp for what lay ahead. The sun was sinking in the sky when the two found one another again. They hurried to finish their work and made their way through the winding streets, just reaching the Red River party as the sun set.

As they stood before the party bound for battle, a murmur rippled through the crowd. Many bowed or inclined their heads in respect. A woman approached and asked, "Why is it that you go to battle bearing no weapon and wearing no armor?"

Crystal and Brant looked at each other sheepishly. In their great preparation they had forgotten to make themselves ready. Crystal drew water from the ground and covered herself in a glossy suit of frozen armor. Brant followed suit, using the earth around him to create a solid shell which enveloped him completely. He heated it with the power he possessed and stood before the crowd in a strong suit of armor, smooth and glistening as new steel. The crowd looked on in awe, their hope restored by the arrival of the Children of the Prophecy. If such powerful magic was with them, success was no longer a dream.

Studying the upturned faces before her, Crystal estimated their numbers to be near five hundred. She addressed them bravely. "I know, to you, our numbers seem small, but we are fighting for what is right and good. You are each powerful in your own way, and we bring our own powers to join in this fight. No matter the outcome, we will march into battle together, and we will emerge victorious!"

The group roared as one, excitement and hope filling their hearts.

Crystal turned at the sound of a familiar voice. "Well done, dear one."

Frinz stood with Zabrina, clad in armor and fighting back tears. She hugged the teens tightly and kissed their foreheads. Zabrina nudged them with her muzzle, whispering softly, "You are the light that will bring us victory. May you be protected and come back safely to us."

The friends embraced, and Brant led Crystal after the group, marching toward the horizon and toward the Red River.

CHAPTER 14
THE ROAD TO BATTLE

The small army trudged toward the Red River in silence. Crystal and Brant could see the uncertainty in the eyes of the men and women who marched around them. This wasn't the way to go, silent and sullen, trapped by fear. Crystal turned to the woman next to her.

"Uh, hello. It's very nice to meet you. My name is Crystal," she said extending her hand.

The woman looked at Crystal oddly, and Crystal realized her mistake. "Oh I'm sorry! Where I come from, we shake hands when we meet new people. I've never had to introduce myself here before. Everyone seems to know who I am. It's just that, well, I just wanted to get to know some people, so that we wouldn't have to be so nervous and—"

The young woman laughed and took Crystal's hand firmly, "Yes, yes, I know well who you are. Who does not know the Children of the Prophecy? I am Seelia."

"Seelia, what a lovely name," Crystal replied, encouraged by the other woman's laugh. "What special ability do you bring to the fight?"

"Nothing very extraordinary," Seelia said, "though I am brave and just as able-bodied as any other in this group. Strong and prepared to fight, am I."

At her proclamation, Crystal blinked, studying her closer. The girl looked to be no older than Crystal or Brant, but was that possible?

"Would it offend you if I ask how old you are?" Crystal asked hesitantly.

Seelia gave another cheerful laugh. "Mercy, no! I am but 16 years old."

Brant, listening nearby, could not help but exclaim, "Really? You're so young to be fighting!"

Seelia tossed her head and answered saucily, "And what has age to do with courage? We fight because we must, for our families and homes. I go to battle so that the old and worn may stay away from war."

"You have brothers and sisters, then?" Brant asked at her mention of family.

"Yes," Seelia answered, her eyes softening as she continued, "I leave behind my two siblings, Kyra and Lafayette, but four years old. For their future, I fight!"

Others took up Seelia's cheer and joined in the conversation speaking of the husbands, children, wives, and other loved ones waiting for them back home. Some talked of past battles and all that they had seen. Time slipped by, and as the river loomed ahead, the small band of warriors talked as though they had known each other a lifetime.

The river stretched before them, a vast expanse of water, no less than a quarter mile wide. The moon, now high in the sky, shone brightly on the water's surface, unable to probe its great depth. The travelers grew quiet until the only sound was that of the rushing water.

Brant turned to the crowd. "I need all of you to stay clear of the river's edge, please. This won't take very long."

At his instruction, the soldiers stepped back. Brant stood facing the river, Crystal at his side. He smiled and lifted his hand to the sky. The earth underfoot began to tremble and mountainous rock formations began to rise from the ground, creating platforms and barriers clustered along the river's edge.

Brant paused to admire his handiwork.

"Showoff," Crystal said, beaming.

He turned to address the crowd once again. "I know it's not perfect, but the rocks will give us cover. The enemy may know where we are by the placement of the barriers, but our archers and catapults can use the cover to take out the front lines before they ever reach us. We'll have an advantage when battle begins."

Crystal continued outlining their plan. "Our catapults require two people to operate each one. We will place them behind the barriers and prepare ourselves for battle, but before we go any further," Crystal paused, smiling mysteriously, "who here is not afraid of water?"

Witches and wizards split from the group, situating themselves behind Brant's walls of rock. Catapults fashioned of ice and stone were placed strategically, and projectiles were fashioned from the water and earth that surrounded their camp. Crystal and Brant lay side by side, staring up at the stars above.

Crystal stretched her hand to the sky. Gathering water from the air, she froze it into dozens of tiny shards which danced in the moonlight. Her hands shook unexpectedly, and she let the ice fall, turning quickly on her side to hide her sudden fear.

Brant sat up, alarmed. "What's wrong, Crystal?"

"Nothing," she whispered quietly.

Brant smoothed her hair, "Please don't keep your feelings to yourself. Won't you tell me what's bothering you?"

Crystal could feel the tears welling, but she forced herself to smile. "Nothing, nothing is wrong. I'm perfectly fine."

Brant frowned and touched Crystal's face. He gently swept him thumb under her eye, catching a tear.

Crystal closed her eyes leaning into his hand, "Just nervous, that's all," she conceded.

"Then tell me," Brant urged.

Nearby, Seelia studied them. "You are close, are you not?" she asked.

Brant swiftly removed his hand from Crystal's face as they looked away, blushing.

Seelia laughed and, turning to her back, sighed. "I miss the one I love. He is in Fotmáre, as part of the reinforcement group that will come to aid us. When he arrives, he and I will fight side by side."

A man sitting on a rock near Seelia joined their musings. "When this battle is over, I am going home to my wife and my children. I miss them dearly, and I long to be with them once more."

Crystal and Brant looked at one another with sad smiles. Their families were so far away, safe and unaware of this land and its struggles.

"Brant, Crystal!" bellowed a man sitting on the ground not far from them. "This is your first battle, no?"

Crystal and Brant nodded silently.

"I offer only this advice. Concentrate on the enemy—not a face or a person—but the enemy at large. Let down your guard, and it will be the last thing you do. You must not think of the people who fall but of the victory that is to come. Slay as many as you can, as fast as you can. That is your only goal."

Seelia nodded her agreement. "Your first battle will not be an easy one, and the fear will grip you as it has each of us. But if you remember the ones for whom you fight, your strength will return. Know that killing is never easy, for if it were, we would be as the enemy is—cold and cruel. Fight for love. Fight for peace. And all will be well in your heart."

Crystal and Brant were silent, lost in thought. They knew they would take lives once the sun came up, and the thought disturbed them greatly. They were charged with protecting people, and they could not ignore their duty.

"Get some rest. You shall require all of your strength, come morning." Seelia told them, as she closed her eyes to find sleep.

Crystal took a deep breath and began her song, her voice dancing through the evening air. The soft tune wove around the camp, calming the men and women making ready for battle. Slowly it built, every note bolstering the resolve of those who listened. The camp quieted and Crystal's tune slowed, its final note echoing in the still night. The soldiers closed their eyes and slept peacefully, thoughts of the battle ahead silenced for the time being.

Talk of any kind ceased as the camp settled in to slumber. The sound of the nearby river was soothing, and Crystal was soon asleep. Brant placed a hand on her heart, feeling its beating, slow and steady, as she slept. His own eyes grew heavy, and he soon joined her in a deep, restful sleep.

Sunrise came all too quickly, and with it, the enemy. Brant and Crystal stood with their troops, hidden by the rocky barriers, willing themselves to remain strong and sure. Brant shifted, his heart pounding, and Crystal took his hand.

"We'll definitely be alright," she assured him.

"Yes. I promise," Brant said.

The thought that this could be their last day, the last day that Crystal would be his, gave Brant courage. Looking deep into her eyes, he saw the deep, powerful love that bound them. He leaned close, whispering for only her ears, "Just in case," and swept her into a passionate embrace. Their kiss spoke the words neither could say, and they clung to that moment, lost to the world around them, for as long as possible. When they parted, Crystal's eyes spoke more than any words ever could.

"There is no, 'just in case.' I know we will walk from this battlefield together," Crystal said, her voice strong and sure. "I love you, Brant, more than anything in this world."

Brant wrapped his arms tightly around Crystal and said, "Me too, Crystal. I love you too—forever."

Hand in hand, they turned to face their fate.

CHAPTER 15
A DAY OF REMEMBRANCE

The soldiers at the Red River watched their enemy approach. Slow and steady they came, line after line of black-clad figures. Before them flew the flag of Sörnam—a black serpent curled into an S and devouring the golden R. The obvious and ominous warning it eschewed was not lost on those awaiting the dark army.

Brant and Crystal made ready for battle, arming themselves with sword and shield. Crystal extended her hand and fashioned an ice sword, shield and helmet. She slipped the helmet over her smooth, blond hair and smiled lovingly at her love, standing bravely beside her. Brant followed suit, and they stayed hidden as the approaching army stopped abruptly.

"What madness is this, Aaliyah?! You promised a flat plain all the way to Keldom!" a man yelled in disgust.

"Quiet, mutt. I did not lie," came the cool reply. "Cease your bothersome chatter, and be on guard. This is obviously a trick. Bring forth the bridge!"

Brant looked at Crystal, and she nodded, looking to the clouds hanging low in the sky. She turned them to solid ice and shattered them into razor-sharp ice crystals. Crystal unleashed the ice shards and watched them plunge to the earth, crushing and slicing through the enemy below.

"NOW!" Brant bellowed.

Four groups jumped from their hiding places and attacked Sürnam's army head on. The remaining groups lay hidden, shooting boulders from the catapults and crushing the screaming enemy across the river. Their ears were filled with the screams of the dying and the battle cries of the living.

Crystal froze a small part of the river, and her band of fighters ran across to attack. Without thought to strategy, Crystal used her blade to slash through the onslaught of enemy fighters, now and again using water drawn from the clouds or river to rain down the sharp, icy shards. Brant threw rocks and moved the ground around them, toppling the enemy even as he slashed at them with his own blade. Crystal saw one of their men fall to the ground with a bloody face. She ran to him, and touched his face. The deep gash closed, and the fallen soldier's eyes flew open

"Thank you kindly," he cried. "The man who hit me shall be dead!"

Crystal cheered and continued to slash her way through the sea of black-armored men and woman. As Sürnam's forces made their way across Crystal's bridge of ice, Crystal melted it, sinking them into the river's depths. More enemy forces advanced toward the river with the makeshift bridge Aaliyah had ordered forward, but Crystal had laid a trap. Hiding beneath the river's dark surface were troops, breathing through the bubble masks Crystal had perfected. As the bridge was laid across the river, they emerged, engulfing it with the flames of a fire spell. Submerging once more, they set about casting spells upon any who neared the river's edge.

Raymond's army fought on, their catapults crushing Sürnam's minions with each blow. They raged on, with every ounce of their strength, beating through the enemy onslaught. Brant fought hard and well, slaying those he came upon and dodging spells and blows against him. Blood seeped from a wound in his shoulder, and he had fallen victim to more than one disorienting spell in the midst of battle. Still, he kept on, always watchful for a glimpse of Crystal. He did not like being away from her in the melee of blood and death.

At the sound of a fearsome roar, Brant turned to see a Mentordor towering over him. It stood twelve feet tall, its body large and clumsy. Its dark scales glistened in the sun, as it stared at Brant victim beady, black eyes. Any trace of the humanity it had once born was gone, and it roared again, the stench of its rotting teeth defiling the air. It raised a monstrous claw into the air, as if to destroy Brant with one blow. Brant only smiled as he brought a small disc of rock to the Mentordor's head, slicing it cleanly off at the neck. Brant laughed and continued to fight his way through the sea of black-armored men and women. All around him, the shouts of spells and incantations could be heard followed by cries of pain and furry. He dodged an oncoming spell as he stabbed a charging soldier.

Crystal slashed through the oncoming enemy, time whirring by as bodies fell at her feet. She moved forward, stopping here and there to heal the others whenever possible. Often, she was too late. Bodies piled around her, and her power was waning. She had stopped healing herself, knowing she would need her strength for the others. Dizzy from the wounds she'd sustained, she fought on, determined not to fall.

I will not stop. Nothing is going to stop me. I'm sure of it! she thought.

Crystal's only warning of the approaching Mentordor was its roar. Before she could turn, its fist collided with her head, shattering her ice helmet and sending her reeling on the ground. Tears spilled from her eyes as she touched the bleeding wound. The battle blurred before her, and then all was silent.

"Brant," she whispered, as she slipped into unconsciousness.

Brant felt a sudden, sharp pain in his head. His heart began to pound as he realized something had happened to Crystal. He looked around franticly to find her, but he was surrounded by Sürnam's soldiers.

"Get out of my way!" Brant shouted.

He swung his sword, and fire burst from it. Those around him fell to the ground, entirely scorched. Brant ran through the flames that now ignited the fields. He ran through the sea of people, his only thought, that of reaching Crystal. Skulls shattered, bodies burned, and Brant slashed on, guided by the force that bound him to her.

He found her laying on the ground, broken and battered, a Mentordor standing over her. A fury beyond anything he could imagine burned inside Brant. Fire spun around him, and with his sword searing red, he ran forward. Leaping through the air, he sliced the Mentordor's head from its body in one swift motion. The dispatched head tumbled to the ground, and the Mentordor's body fell limp and lifeless. Brant scooped Crystal up in his arms, praying with all of his might that she was still alive.

A band of enemy soldiers charged toward Brant. He turned and stared, his eyes burning red with fury. Fire still danced around him as he held Crystal's lifeless form. The flames burst forth, burning all that surrounded him. He watched the enemy perish in his flame.

Brant stood on a rock and levitated it, letting it carry him across the river. He reached the barriers where one of the healers rested. Brant set Crystal down, his eyes steely and hard. The healer studied the wound grimly then began muttering incantations over the gaping wound. As the wound stitched itself together, Crystal stirred.

"Brant?" she whispered softly.

"I'm here. It's ok. You're safe."

"No, I wanted to kill it," she said with a weak smile.

Brant laughed. "I'm going back out there. They need me."

Crystal stood slowly, her eyes adjusting once more. "I'm going too!"

Brant put a hand on her shoulder. "Please, stay here, Crystal. You need to rest."

"I'm not going to rest while others are dying. I can't let these people just die," Crystal said. She smiled and stretched her hand to the sky, and her eyes changed to an icy blue, something Brant had never seen before. Every cloud floating in the sky turned to ice crystals and began to rain down on the army.

She froze a line of water, and they ran quickly across, striking down the enemy in their path. The enemy was setting up what looked like canons along the river bank. They fired hooks with ropes attached, which burrowed into the rocky cliffs. The soldiers began climbing the ropes in an attempt to cross the river.

Those who were hiding in the water cut the ropes by throwing knives or swords. Crystal's hidden water warriors were affective. Those clinging to the ropes fell and sank into the river. Some tried to remove their armor to avoid sinking, but those who had been hiding in the water attacked and killed them, letting the bodies sink to the bottom of the river.

Aaliyah watched her forces move forward and fall back, over and over, like the tide waxing and waning. With every setback, her patience diminished. They had underestimated the forces of Raymond's feeble army, and now they were paying in loss of life and time. *Raymond*, Aaliyah thought, and a wicked smile crept across her lips.

She turned to her guards. "I grow tired of watching these underlings lose to such meager forces. May you all meet your death. I care not. I have much to do in the name of our master."

With that, she called on her darkest magic and disappeared from the field of battle. Her guards looked about them then ran into battle.

Crystal and Brant stopped, breathing heavily and battle weary. They were surrounded by the enemy. None of their companions were in sight.

With the river close by, Crystal smiled. "I'll take this half if you take yours?"

"Sure thing," Brant said.

Crystal pulled water from the river, froze it into a million tiny shards of ice, and ran them through the surrounding army. She watched as they fell to the ground, defeated.

Brant stretched out his hand, and out of the ground shot thousands of spikes.

Once Crystal and Brant finished the enemy before them, they moved on. As they slashed through more and more of Sürnam's forces, they saw less and less of their own. Crystal looked up and saw that the remaining Mentordor had crossed the river. Crystal could see them smashing the catapults, their large hands sending Raymond's army flying. Two stood in the water, killing the last of the soldiers hidden there.

"No!" Crystal shouted, running to the river's edge in an attempt to save them.

Sürnam's army was making its way across the river, decimating all in its path.

Crystal and Brant watched, alone on the other side of the river, as the dark army moved forward to the small band of fighters hiding behind the barriers.

Crystal stretched out her hand, freezing the entire river in an instant. She snapped her fingers and ice broke from the river and snapped the bridges. She melted the ice, letting those who remained drown in the river's depths.

She once again froze a small ice bridge, and darted toward the other side of the river where those she had sworn to protect were dying. Brant shot spikes of solid rock from the mountains into the remaining Mentordor, and they lifelessly tumbled to the ground. Crystal slashed through the enemy who stood between her and the rock barriers. Brant followed, flinging rocks and piercing hearts of his foes. He snapped his fingers and the men surrounding him burst into flame. They ran from him, screaming, seeking relief for their burning flesh.

"Brant! Lower the mountains so we can see! Be careful. Some of our friends might still be hiding!" Crystal shouted above the sound of battle.

Brant did so, slowly lowering the mountains into the earth. He had to concentrate and took his time. Once the barriers were lowered, Brant and Crystal continued on. Crystal's eyes darted back and forth as she swung her sword, cutting down those in her path. They continued to search but saw none that they knew. Brant lit the grass under their feet, and everything they could see was engulfed in flames.

Crystal shattered the ice that remained from her bridge and cast the shards into the air, letting them slice through those who remained standing on the decimated plain. She stopped, breathing heavily, listening for the sounds of their brothers in arms. Brant stood beside her. They heard nothing but the roaring flames that surrounded them. Brant snapped his fingers, and the fire extinguished. A thick layer of smoke hung in the air around them, and Crystal blew a gust of wind around the battle field until the smoke cleared.

They froze. The banks of the river lay strewn with the bodies of the dead. None moved; none breathed. Crystal and Brant stared at each other in horror. They had done what they must to win the battle, but none had lived to share in their victory.

CHAPTER 16

MISFORTUNES OF WAR

T ears streamed down Crystal's face as she turned to Brant. "Why? I… I thought… maybe…"

Brant looked at her, his eyes brimming. He gently brushed Crystal's cheek with his hand, the grime and blood of battle mingling with her sadness.

"Maybe…" Crystal said softly.

Brant looked deep inter her eyes, willing her to tell him where her thoughts lay. Then suddenly, he knew.

Crystal stared blindly ahead and whispered, "Maybe…I-I can bring them back. Heal them…"

She turned back to where her friends had fallen and stopped only when Brant gripped her arm. Looking into his eyes, reality and reason returned. He shook his head, and she collapsed against him.

Crystal's eyes widened as shock set in. Her frozen armor melted, leaving her wet and weary.

"They were our friends! They had lives and families and loved ones waiting back home!"

Crystal recalled Seelia's stories of her twin siblings awaiting her return and the lover on his way to assist her in battle. Brant removed his own armor with a snap of his fingers and sank to his knees beside a weeping Crystal, wrapping her in his arms.

"They knew what this mission held… We all did." Brant said as they sobbed together.

"I… I couldn't… save them," Crystal wept, fighting the sense of failure threatening to swallow her whole.

"We did all we could… Crystal… I …I hope that… they would understand… and be happy that we finished the battle… I hope… they don't think… we failed them."

The sun was setting over the grisly battle field. Lifeless bodies littered the bloodstained grass, and everywhere was the smoke and stench of war. Brant and Crystal remained where they were, holding each other tightly. They stirred for nothing, even as the sound of footsteps fell behind them.

Zabrina stepped forward, breaking through the silence. Neither acknowledged her presence, even as she sat next to them and nuzzled them comfortingly.

"You did all that you could. This is no failure. The battle has been won, and our loved ones waiting at home have been spared."

Her words echoed in the sadness and silence around them. They knew she was right, that the people who had perished fighting alongside them had died protecting those they loved. Crystal and Brant would not let their friends perish in vain. Without a word, they embraced their dragon friend, overcome by exhaustion and grief.

"Come, little ones. Let us go home."

As Crystal and Brant climbed to Zabrina's back, a man approached them, a look of utter despair upon his face.

"Please," the man began, "Seelia. Did she? Is she really?" Tears welled in his eyes and fell on the very ground where his love had lost her life.

Crystal ran forward and hugged the man.

"Yes. She spoke of you and of her siblings. She loved you. She loved you very much, and she could not wait to… to fight by your side… sorry… We're so sorry…" Crystal's words dissolved in sobs.

The man collected himself and spoke, his voice shaking with sadness, "We knew that, when we entered this war together, one of us may not make it out alive. We… we p-promised one another that, i-if that were to happen, we would not mourn… for long."

Crystal squeezed the young man's shoulder in sympathy. "I'm sorry," she whispered.

The boy shook his head, and despite the tears that continued to fall, he smiled.

"You must not be sorry, Children of the Prophecy. You have fought hard and won well. Those who died have died with great honor."

The young man bowed as Crystal climbed onto Zabrina's back, eager to leave the horrors of battle behind. As they flew away, Crystal fell asleep to the sound of Brant's questions.

"Zabrina," he said, his voice raspy with tears, "what about the rest? Where are they? And Frinz?"

"Those below will remain here, and dispose of the dead. We will honor them properly once we are all together. Frinz is tending to greater needs in Keldom, but all of this I will explain later. For now, young one, you must recover."

Brant rested his head on Zabrina's neck. Closing his eyes, he felt the weight of his grief begin to lessen, replaced with the heaviness of deep, undreaming sleep.

Zabrina smiled sadly. "I am deeply sorry, little ones. I did not know this would be so difficult for you, nor did I suspect you would be this ill prepared. For that, I am deeply sorry."

Zabrina flew swiftly to the camp at Keldom where a grief-stricken Frinz awaited her. "What is wrong, my friend?" the dragon asked concernedly.

"Raymond… was murdered." Frinz sobbed, her voice muffled by grief. "I left Arron with his father in the tent, and when I returned, Raymond was dead."

"Far too many lives have been lost today, my dearest friend," Zabrina sighed.

Frinz wiped the tears from her face and looked at Crystal and Brant, still sleeping on Zabrina's back. "How… how are they?"

"Exhausted, but otherwise unharmed. They had a small number of wounds, but I have already tended to them. For now, I will remain here and let them sleep."

"What about everyone else?" Frinz asked.

Zabrina looked away, "None but these two survived."

CHAPTER 17

UNWANTED DEATH

It was close to noon the next day before Crystal and Brant woke. They found themselves in a tent, Zabrina nearby keeping watch.

"Are you awake?" the dragon asked in a gentle voice.

"Yes, thank you." Crystal said politely, her voice raspy from the stress of battle.

Brant awoke to Crystal's words. His heart ached to see the dark, weary circles under her eyes. "Where is Frinz?" he asked, looking about for their friend.

"She has joined the others in honoring Raymond. His life was taken yesterday…by Aaliyah. When the winds of battle turned against her army, she stole away, ever the coward, and was able to sneak through our forces and kill Raymond. I am saddened by his loss but so thankful that she had no chance to come for either of you or Frinz."

Crystal and Brant cringed at her words, though they knew them to be true.

"You're right." Crystal said, wincing at the soreness in her muscles as she stood from the cot. "If we had died, there would be little hope for this war… Brant… I know that right now, we both feel like we failed the people we went to battle with yesterday, but we can't let that stop us. If we do, we will lose this war and fail this land and its people."

Crystal offered Brant a hand and a renewed smile. "So let's do our best together."

Brant clasped her hand and rose from his bed. The battle had taken its toll on their bodies as well as their spirits.

"We will stay, only to honor those who have fallen, but must immediately depart after. We must take you home right away. You need rest and strength for what is yet to come. Frinz will remain here to continue her work. It must be so, for now."

They walked the somber city streets, quiet with mourning. All gathered at the center, where an enormous pile of worn shoes towered before them.

Seeing the teenagers confused glances, Zabrina replied, "We each leave a pair of shoes as tribute, to carry those who passed onto the next life."

The pair removed the shoes from their feet and gingerly added them to the pile. From all around came hushed cries of thanks and grateful embraces. The townspeople waved their hands in unison, and the shoes burst into beautiful, green flames. The smoke carried to the sky, honoring the brave fallen heroes.

Crystal and Brant studied one another, wishing they could stay and speak with Arron. Still, Zabrina and Frinz knew best.

Crystal turned to Zabrina. "We are ready to leave. We must rest and be ready for what is next to come."

Arron stood in the council tent, staring at the place where his father had fallen. Hard as he tried, he could not block the memory of his father's death. Aaliyah came and went, in an instant, teleporting to the very spot where his father stood and leaving just as quickly. The sound of her death spell had lingered in the air. Arron rushed to his father's side, but all that remained was the great man's lifeless body.

Arron shook himself out of his trance. The world around him moved on, and so must he. He had no family left. All had gone before him. Arron's mother had died when he was but a child of ten. He had sat by his mother's deathbed, watching over her in those final hours. Her last words to her son were a whisper of encouragement.

"Do your best, my boy, and know that I am proud of you, always."

She had dismissed him then to whisper her final words to her husband before passing on. Arron knew Raymond was with her now, behind the veil of death, at peace once more.

As tears clouded his eyes, Arron felt a gentle touch on his shoulder. He turned to see Frinz, her eyes pools of sympathy. Before she could speak, he wrapped her in a tight embrace.

"Thank you," Arron said softly, "thank you for always being here for me. You're... the only one I have left... Thank you, Frinz."

They clung tightly to one another, unwilling to break their embrace for fear of falling apart.

Zabrina flew swiftly toward Mardra's cottage, eager to deliver Crystal and Brant into its protective boundaries. She could feel a change in her young charges and knew that the battle had forged a stronger bond between the two. Crystal and Brant woke as they landed, still weary and bleary-eyed from their ordeal.

"Are we here, already?" Crystal asked.

"We must be," Brant said, stretching. "Come on, let's hurry. There's so much to tell Mardra." Both Crystal and Zabrina nodded in agreement.

As they walked, Crystal studied Brant. The sun shone down on his dark locks, and Crystal couldn't help but think how handsome Brant truly was. She was lucky in so many ways.

Crystal took Brant's hand and leaned against him as they walked along. Zabrina beamed, at the pair. When they reached the burnt door, Mardra was waiting for them. She ran to greet the trio, with open arms.

"I'm so very glad that you are both safe... but where is my daughter?"

Zabrina answered quietly, "She has stayed behind with Arron. His father's life was taken, and Frinz is his only comfort."

Mardra's eyes fell to the ground, "You are right. It is best for him, poor boy. He has been through so much." Mardra smiled slightly, "But I am sure, if I know my daughter, she will make his aching heart whole once more."

They made their way indoors and found a delicious meal spread before them. Between bites, Brant and Crystal told of the battle and their losses. Mardra's face fell as she learned that there were no other survivors.

She looked up at the end of their story and asked, "Are you both... alright?"

"Yes," answered Brant, taking Crystal's hand, "tired, but alright."

"We realize that we mustn't let the others die in vain. We owe them, and all the people of Thurnangl, our best. If we are to reach the end of this war, then we must take courage and fight!" Crystal said with great confidence.

Mardra smiled, marveling at how much they had grown in such a short time. Brant stood and cleared the empty plates from the table. Returning, he took Crystal's hand.

"Would you mind if the two of us went for a walk?" he asked Mardra.

Mardra smiled kindly and replied, "No, not at all. Just come back safely."

The door had scarcely closed behind them when Mardra turned to Zabrina. "I feel a little sad that I missed what has passed between those two. It must have been a divine moment."

"If nothing else, I am sure that is true." Zabrina said.

Gazing down the hall after them, her face grew solemn. "I believe we must take them to visit Mangö. The time has come to speak with Drinin."

Mardra nodded. "That is for the best. We will need all the help we can muster."

"And if what I predict is true, Mardra, we will need their help desperately."

Outside, the afternoon sun peeked through the trees above Crystal and Brant, brightening the day. Brant brought Crystal's hand to his face, leaning into its warmth.

"I love you," Crystal whispered, their troubles momentarily forgotten. Stretching to her toes, she leaned in to kiss him.

CHAPTER 18
A PAST LONG FORGOTTEN

"WHAT?!" Sürnam screamed, furious at the news Aaliyah brought. The guards around him jumped.

Aaliyah's cold, dead eyes held no fear or remorse as she recounted their loss in battle. "Your armies fell, unsuccessful. Crystal and Brant have escaped with their lives."

Sürnam's hands shook as he fought to contain his rage.

Aaliyah continued with a cruel smile. "But I have news that will please you, my lord. Raymond is dead by my hands."

Sürnam considered her words then laughed harshly. "Well, well. That wasn't part of our plan."

"The fool army was losing, and there was no recourse but to strike while I could. And what a blow we have struck," Aaliyah said, stepping closer.

"This does please me," cackled Sürnam, leaning in ever so closely as Aaliyah's cold eyes drank in his dark face.

Sürnam's attention was held by the story of Raymond's death, and he paid no mind to the lovely woman who crept from his throne room, heart heavy. At nineteen, Lilly was as kind and beautiful as

Sürnam was vicious. She radiated light in his court of darkness. She was neither slave nor ally but bore the distinction of being something much harder to bear. She was his sister.

Sürnam was born to a loving mother and father who wanted nothing more than to raise a child of strength and courage. Young and in love, they had married and settled in their small village of Coppertown. When they were blessed with their first child, they were overjoyed.

His father named him Sürnam and turned to the midwife with a smile. "A good strong name it is, strong enough for our special boy."

The midwife rejoiced with the couple. Her happiness turned to unease as she looked upon the face of the child. "His eyes are as black as pitch," she said with a gasp.

The baby's parents were undisturbed by this anomaly, blinded by their love for their newborn child. They knew only the joy of parenthood.

Happiness was fleeting for the family, who soon learned that more than the baby's eyes were black. He was a baby in name alone, wreaking havoc in the lives of all who were near. Furnishings in the home would burst into flame with a mere glance from the child, and his parents were often scorched when his wishes were not granted. More often than not, it took every ounce of the young parents' strength to keep their home from being destroyed. The excuses used to explain away his behavior soon fell on deaf ears. Whispers of what the child truly was could not be hushed. His parents were forced to avoid the company of others and hide from their friends and neighbors.

As Sürnam grew, so did the dark magic inside him. He could command others to do his bidding and had neither the conscience nor the kindness to keep his powers in check. None in the village had ever seen such power before, and they were more than a little terrified of the black-eyed boy and his new, dark magic. Try as they might, his parents could not keep him from doing harm.

One morning, as his parents slept, a seven-year-old Sürnam crept from the house. He walked down the street until he came upon his neighbor's pet, batting around a tiny insect. The furry animal gazed at Sủrnam as he approached, its ears twitching at a perceived threat. The young boy laughed mirthlessly and muttered a single word, "Hentach."

Its eyes widened, and the tiny creature fell to the ground, lifeless. Sủrnam chuckled darkly at his newfound magic. He had created a successful death spell. His heart swelled with the power he now wielded, and he moved down the street, eager to find new victims.

There was a small boy, just a little younger than Sủrnam, playing in a nearby garden. The little boy stopped and glanced at Sủrnam.

"Good morning!" The boy said excitedly.

Sủrnam only stared at the boy as he walked towards him.

"I have not seen you here before. What is your name?" the boy asked.

Sủrnam stared silently; then a wicked smile stretched across his face.

The boy's gleeful expression turned to confusion, "What is so funny?"

Sủrnam put his hand inches from the boy's face. The boy blinked, still confused, ignorant of the danger that stood before him.

"Erentor," Sủrnam whispered icily.

The boy's smile faded, and his face grew pale. His mind unable to shake the dark magic, the air whooshed from his lungs. His pupils widened, and his eyes grew dull and lifeless. The boy's tiny body fell backward, hitting the ground with thud. A chuckle escaped Sủrnam's lips.

Screams brought the villagers into the street where a woman lay sobbing, her lifeless son in her arms.

"Lynton! Lynton!" she wept, rocking the tiny boy who would never again open his eyes.

Neighbors comforted her, holding her hands and as hysteria took over. They could understand little of what she said, but one word was clear. "Sủrnam"

By the time Sörnam's name had spread through the frightened village, the evil young boy was long gone. He knew of only one place where he might grow his magic and practice evil deeds. By the time he set foot in the dark land of Garzula, word of his power had reached them. They welcomed him graciously, knowing him as the boy of pure darkness, the one touched by evil.

Making his way to Palmer, the ruler of Garzula's forces, Sörnam pronounced himself ready to fight. Palmer was a fearsome leader, and his astonishment at the boy's proclamation was tempered by his desire to use Sörnam in his war of hate and greed.

Sörnam grew, more powerful by the year. He was but fifteen years old when Palmer brought him up through the ranks. Where once was an evil little boy, now stood a young man with the power to take life, and no one to stop him. He became invaluable, the ultimate executioner.

The boy who had walked away from Coppertown was but a shell of the formidable teen who returned. He had honed his craft. Now Sörnam would exact his revenge on those who had locked him away from the world. He would vanquish his parents first, and the townspeople would be lucky if he spared a single one.

He found the tiny house little changed from his childhood. Hidden by morning shadows, he looked through the window at the lovely scene inside. Sitting by the hearth were his parents, and they were not alone. In his mother's arms was a tiny infant wrapped in pink swaddling. A sudden rage overtook him as he studied the baby, and a new plan sprung to his mind. He would make them suffer in ways they never imagined.

Sörnam blasted through the front door and stood before his parents. At the sight of him, they recoiled in horror, and his father moved forward to shield the baby and her mother from the monster before them.

"Leave this place!" his father cried. "There is no place for you here. We seek peace!"

Sörnam's words sliced through the room. "Do you think I came to stay? I have but one intention before I reduce this place to a pile of rubble. You will die knowing that your daughter is with me, forever."

His mother stood her ground. "You shall not hurt our precious Lilly!" she shouted.

Sörnam snapped his fingers, and the baby floated from her mother's arms into Sörnam's.

Sörnam watched his parents lunge for the baby. They came quickly toward him, but his magic was strong and infused with the hate he bore. With Lilly safely in his arms, he spoke the incantation and watched his parents fall.

"Amzelo!"

The pair before him writhed in pain, a scorching fire running through their veins. It ended almost as suddenly as it had begun, and the pair succumbed to his punishment.

They lay before him, dead on the floor, and Sörnam smiled down at their limp bodies. With that, he walked from the house. A single whisper from his lips, and the house was engulfed in flames. There would be nothing but rubble and ash for the neighbors to find.

Sörnam returned to Garzula, intent on power. The baby in his care had come as a surprise, but he relished at the thought of raising her in the ways of his evil kin, stripping all that was good and kind from her. She would learn from the castle staff and grow to know Phärnam as her true home. Thurnangl would be no more to her than a place whose people and lands must be conquered.

Months went by, and Sörnam waited, his plans set. He saw his sixteenth birthday come and go, ushering in yet another victory. For Palmer "mysteriously" grew gravely ill. Upon the army leader's death, Sörnam was granted power over the thrown. His power heightened, his rank undisputed, Sörnam began his reign of terror.

His changes were far-reaching and swift, leaving little as it had been before. The flag of Palmer's rule was removed, and in its place flew a new crest—a giant serpent devouring its prey. The people succumbed to his command, and blackness shrouded the land. Gone were the days of free thought and loyalty. All that remained was a terrible, gripping fear.

Sürnam raised Lilly on lies, feeding her deception that kept her bound to him. She thought her brother a great hero who had saved her from the abuse of a loveless home. Her gratitude knew no bounds, and though he could not comprehend her love, it bound her to him and allowed him complete control. That control turned into obsession, and Sürnam soon possessed feelings that were those of a man for a woman.

Lilly grew, sheltered from the world at large. She spent many hours reading and wondering the castle. Within its walls, she discovered the great magic she possessed and was proud to show her brother the spells she had mastered. Her talent was remarkable, and she matched Sürnam himself in potential.

Often left alone, Lilly loved to explore the castle and the secrets it held. At the age of thirteen, she was enjoying one such excursion when she came across two maids speaking in hushed tones.

"—and that is why she lives here, locked away from the world."

Another voice replied "To think he murdered his own parents, and right in front of the girl too, though she would not remember. She was but a tiny thing. He has a sick and twisted heart full of unnatural feelings for Lilly. I fear for her."

"There is truly a sickness in him, but we must not speak of it. The walls have ears. I only hope she finds escape from his twisted, evil grasp before it is too late."

The book Lilly held fell unnoticed to the floor as her hands trembled violently. She tried to grasp all she had heard.

It could be a lie…silly gossip…that is all. But so many do fear my brother, and he is so powerful…. But our parents… and he…he could not really…

Seeking answers, Lilly rushed to her brother's throne room and burst through the doors.

"Lilly, my pet, to what do we owe this pleasure?" Sörnam's voice was measured and calm as though eyeing his prey.

Lilly cringed at his voice. "Do not…is it true? Our parents…you killed them…is it TRUE?"

Sörnam smiled as though they were speaking of the weather.

"Those wretched creatures that locked me away from the world, ashamed of my power? Why yes, I did. Why do you ask?"

Lilly remained silent, her body trembling as she gained the courage to ask her next question. "Why did you save me? Why was I spared?"

His answer chilled her to her core. "It's simple, my sweet. Because I thought to ruin you, but now I must possess you instead. Keep you as only my own."

Before Lilly could stop herself she asked, "Are you in love with me?"

Sörnam laughed coldly and walked slowly toward Lilly. Tears were running down her face, and her head was spinning.

"If that is what you wish to call it, then yes," he said in an icy voice.

Lilly could only whisper through her revulsion, "You are sick… sick and twisted…and unnatural."

Sörnam's rage overpowered him, and he clutched her wrist in his vicelike grip. His words were quiet and deadly. "You are alive because I choose to keep you that way. You will remain so until you come to understand my feelings and reciprocate. Trust me, child, you WILL obey me."

He leaned in close, his grip tightening on her, his hot breath rancid upon her lips.

Gone was any affection she had felt for the brother who was her only kin. Lilly jerked away from his grasp with all of her might. She spat her reply, disdain dripping from every word.

"You are my blood. Is your heart so twisted that you cannot see your own error? I will never be yours, NEVER!"

Lilly ran from the ugly, vile thoughts of her brother and did not stop until she had reached her quarters, high in a castle turret. There she would remain as the days and years passed by, too disgusted to venture near her brother again. Sörnam never followed, and she was left to wait and wonder. There she remained, year after year. From her window, she could see the far away mountains and gaze upon the evening stars. She sat and waited, knowing deep within that her true purpose awaited.

CHAPTER 19
A BEACON OF LIGHT

Lilly's opportunity came when she was nineteen. Long had she plotted her escape—tried again and again—but was always thwarted, brought to the feet of the very evil that ruled her life. Finally, the conditions were right, and her heart was prepared.

The guards were changing shifts, when she climbed from her tower window, quickly and quietly, and made her way through the palace. At every turn, new danger lurked, but her years of solitude had made her familiar with the castle's secrets, and she used them to her advantage. She reached the outermost castle wall, and quietly recited an incantation. An enormous boulder moved with ease, creating a gap large enough for her escape. When finally she had cleared the outer wall of the castle, she turned to look back at her prison. No person followed. No shouts or alarms met her ears. She had escaped, or so she thought.

Three days she ran, barely stopping to rest or eat. On and on she fled—to where and what, she did not know. She ran from her past, from the cruelty and evil that had so consumed her brother and all he ruled. She came upon the city of Keldom and was grateful for its vastness. Here, she could blend in and disappear. Running low on food and carrying no money, she wondered the streets, contemplating her fate.

Lilly found herself in good fortune on her first day in the city as she walked along, trying her best to blend in. Nearby, a fruit cart crashed to the ground toppling the beautiful fruit it carried to the ground. Lilly ran to offer her assistance. "Please, let me help you," she said.

As she knelt to recover the fallen fruit, a strong voice met her ears. "You are truly kind, ma'am."

Lilly looked up into brilliant eyes the color of a sunset in the handsomest face she had ever beheld. She was taken aback by the man's hulking frame and gentle smile. She blushed nervously, dropping the fruit she had just retrieved.

The young man chuckled at her embarrassment, thinking her the sweetest thing he'd ever laid eyes on.

"Thank you for helping a poor stranger. I am much obliged. My name is Basem. Might I know the name of my savior?"

Lilly blinked and remained silent momentarily, but then she smiled the faintest of smiles.

"It's very nice to meet you. My name is Lilly."

Together, they placed the fruits back onto the cart and began to walk down the street.

"Is this cart yours?" she asked.

"No. It is my father's. We grow fruit in our garden to sell in the city. It is a good business, when the fruit is in good condition." Basem sighed as he studied the bruised and dirty produce.

Lilly was eager to be near him, and before she could stop herself, she suggested, "Might I help you clean the fruit? We could wash it and make it beautiful again. I am sure you would sell every last piece!"

Lilly's heart thudded as she awaited his answer.

Basem smiled the tenderest of smiles and offered his arm. "Nothing would please me more."

Basem escorted Lilly to his home, a small house on the edge of the city. The house's size belied the wonders that it held, for the backyard was a sight to behold. Garden rows filled the center, and a grove of orchard trees stood tall and fruitful around the perimeter. Lilly gazed around in wonder as Basem brought forth a water basin and began to gently scrub the fruit.

"My mother was gifted the ability to grow and tend plants of every shape and size." Basem said, love for his mother evident in his face. "She has an amazing talent, and it has served us well in business. She tends our crops and my father manages the business. I help where I can."

Lilly grinned at the cart of fruit and whispered a spell, rendering the fruit beautiful and pristine once more. Basem gasped and thanked her, bewildered at the caliber of her magic.

"Do you have a special gift as well?" Lilly asked.

"I do not believe so. I am told my kindness is a magical quality, but I think that a bit unlikely. Kindness does not rely on magic but on the heart. I have never been skillful at magic, but I get by." Basem's smile and thoughtfulness left Lilly momentarily speechless.

His voice and manner took her breath away. His aura shown with kindness and generosity of spirit, and Lilly felt herself opening her heart to him. She had never been shown true kindness before.

"Would you stay for lunch?" he asked her.

Lilly blushed. "No, no, thank you. I should not overstay my welcome."

"Please," Basem pleaded gently, taking her hand in his, "stay." His eyes pierced her soul and rendered her helpless.

Lilly only nodded. Basem eagerly lead her to the house.

The house was small and simple, nothing out of the ordinary, but to Lilly it was magnificent. They entered through the garden door, and Lilly found herself in a cozy kitchen. Looking about, she marveled at the pots bubbling on the stove and the smells of wonderful food about her.

Basem led her into a living room with worn couches and a lived-in look about it. A staircase rose from the corner to a second floor where, Basem told her, were tucked three tiny bedrooms. Lilly felt an unexplainable peace and breathed in the aura of a real home.

"Mother, I'm home, and I brought a friend as well!" Basem called, leading Lilly back to the kitchen.

Lilly looked up in surprise. She had never been called friend before. It was a wonderful feeling, and Lilly couldn't help but beam.

A beautiful woman bustled down the stairs, her curly, crimson hair falling in wisps about her face. Kind eyes, the color of golden flames, smiled down at Lilly from a face whose beauty was untouched by age.

"Well hello! Pleasure to meet you, my dear. You are in luck, for I always make too much food for the three of us." she stepped forward, taking Lilly's hands in her own.

Lilly bowed. "It is a pleasure to meet you, ma'am. My name is Lilly."

"A name to match such a sweet face," the woman cooed. "Well, my name is Karima, and you are quite welcome at our table."

"Basem are you back so soon?" called a man as he swept down the stairs.

"Father, I would like you to meet Lilly. Lilly, this is my father, Calictus."

Calictus bowed deeply, his striking yellow eyes fixed on the lovely guest before him. He swept a large hand through his silver hair and said cordially, "It is very nice to meet you, Lilly. How did you come to acquaint yourself with Basem?"

"Oh I was clumsy and knocked over the cart, and Lilly helped me salvage our fare. She offered to help me sell it as well." Basem laughed, feeling foolish.

"Well that was truly generous, Lilly. Thank you very much."

The lunch that Karima made was far better fare Lilly had ever tasted. Every morsel was fresh, grown and picked from their backyard.

As they ate, they spoke of Basem's clumsiness. He had been so all his life. Lilly was amazed at their kindness, and for the first time, felt at peace. When they asked where Lilly hailed from, she answered simply that she lived very far away and did not intend to go back. Sensing her reluctance to speak of her past, Basem excused them from the table and led Lilly outside.

"I am sorry. It was not our place to pry into your past. That is your own life." Basem apologized.

"You have shown me such kindness. I have never even met my parents or been with people who were so kind. It is a wonderful feeling to know people so full of goodness," Lilly said sadly.

Basem took her hand impulsively. "Well, why not stay here—with us—for a while. It seems you have no other place to go, and," he touched her face gently, "it might help heal your troubled heart."

Lilly blushed, her eyes brimming with tears at his gesture.

Lilly stayed with Basem's family, spending her days at the fruit cart—sometimes with Basem, sometimes alone. People were drawn to her, and few left the cart without an armful of fresh fruit when Lilly was the vendor. Basem watched her happiness blossom.

Every morning they would go out with a full cart and return when it was empty. She loved to see Basem smile and laugh. They grew closer as the weeks wore on, and Lilly became part of their family. They were happiest when they were together, each delighting in the other's smile and always working to please each other.

Happiness was fleeting for Lilly, and her time with Basem was soon to end. As they walked home from market one evening, Lilly sensed a shadow following close behind. Her nervousness grew, and her fears were realized when she saw a familiar face in a nearby alley. Sörnam's spies had found her at last. The color drained from her face, and she began to tremble. Basem saw her distress and stopped in his tracks, his eyes full of questions.

Pulling Basem into a nearby niche, Lilly finally let herself fall apart.

"What is wrong?" he asked, touching her face.

Lilly looked away from him, "I–I have to leave now," she said, her voice shaking. "I am sorry."

Basem cupped her face in his hands and looked deeply into her eyes.

"It is alright. You can tell me." He paused at the sadness in her eyes. "Nothing, nothing is going to change my love for you."

Tears poured from Lilly's eyes as she told him of her past. Never once did Basem let go of her or show fear as she told of her relation to Sörnam. When she told him of Sörnam's wicked love for her, Basem raged silently, but still he held her.

"I have to leave and run. I will not let him find me here. I do not want him to find you and hurt you. Basem, I love you too much to let you be harmed!" She buried her face in his chest and he wrapped his arms tightly around her.

"Hush now," Basem whispered. "You will not run. We will do away with that spy, and Sörnam will never learn that you are here."

Lilly held him close. "Surly the spy is not alone, they rarely are. A commotion of death would surly attract a kind of attention that would cost many lives here."

Basem hugged her tightly, and sighed. "Then what are we going to do? Something has to be done," he said.

"I will go willingly, so no one is to get hurt," Lilly said boldly, though her body was full of fear. The very thought of going back to Sörnam sent chills up her spine.

Basem tightened his arms around her, tears glistening in his golden eyes. "I do not wish for you to leave, Lilly. I cannot allow you go back to that place," His voice shook with sadness, and Lilly's heart ached.

"I must go, Basem. Sörnam will think nothing of destroying this city, of killing its people, all to acquire his desire. I have lasted in his keep this long, I must return, if only to spare the lives of these people. You cannot fight him, for that will mean death. Please, let me go."

Basem's heart crumbled at the weight of her words. How could he lose her? But how could he keep her and not be responsible for thousands of lost lives?

"We will see each other again, Lilly. This is not the end. You must know that. I cannot let you go if you do not know that I would fight for you—to the death."

"Yes, my love. Everything will be alright. That, I know for certain," Lilly whispered, pulling away from the safety of his embrace.

How was it that the one person, the one thing she found that needed her, was being taken away now?

Basem wiped away her tears. "Our love will keep us together. Nothing shall ever truly separate us. I will never leave you for my heart is now with you."

Basem kissed Lilly passionately, clinging to the moment. They stayed, pressed close to one another, neither willing to part. But Lilly knew she must break away. Mustering a smile, Lilly stepped back and looked deep into his eyes.

"I love you. Never give up, and do not forget me."

Basem took her hand and kissed it. "How could a man ever forget the one he loves?"

Lilly kissed him once more and walked away letting her hand slowly slip out of his.

Lilly's return to Phärnam was swift. She knew the way, and she knew what she must do. She settled into her room and awaited the summons from Sörnam. When at last it came, Lilly took a deep breath, put on her bravest face, and went to the throne room. She bowed stiffly in front of Sörnam.

"You have had quite the time, have you not?" Sörnam hissed as she stood before his throne awaiting her punishment. He brought his hand hard across her face, with such force that his guards stepped back in fear.

Yes she thought, *punish me. As long as he is safe and happy, I care not what happens to me.* Tears of pain ran down Lilly's face.

"How dare you leave this place and disobey me. Did you think we would not find you? You thought you could live there happily with HIM did you?"

Lilly's heart stopped. She couldn't speak.

"I will personally make sure that you learn your lesson. I will burn Keldom to the ground and kill every living, breathing person who stands. There will be no one to go back to. There is nothing you can do."

"No please!!!" Lilly begged, "Please punish me, not them!"

"I am punishing you!" Sörnam yelled at the top of his voice. His words echoed through the immense room. "Rest assured, with every lifeless body, you will feel your punishment."

Sörnam leaned close to Lilly and whispered in her ear. "There will be no one left for you to love but me."

Lilly's heart burned with fury and revulsion. "I will never love a sick and disgusting THING like you,"

Sörnam merely laughed icily, striking her once more. He sat back on his throne and waved his hand. A guard escorted Lilly to her room. Lilly was truly captive. Guards were posted at her door, morning and night. There was no way for her to save the people she loved.

Two months passed, and Lilly could only listen to Sörnam's vile plots of revenge against the people of Keldom. Her heart shrank and she weakened as she heard of his troops marching to battle. She longed for word of the battle's outcome, but none met her ears. The maids became, once more, a revealing light in her dark prison. She overheard their whispers of a Prophecy and the saviors that had come to fulfill it. There was talk of a stale mate in battle.

She had evaded her guards and crept to the throne room, entering through the barely opened door to see her brother in a rage. Sörnam's forces had been pushed back, but Keldom had suffered a great blow as well. In his anger and disappointment, Lilly found her hope. She knew Basem must surely be alive. Her heart would tell her otherwise.

Sörnam no longer spoke to Lilly, nor did he call her to his throne room. She had escaped his notice that day that she'd crept in to hear him rail against Aaliyah, and she knew he was too much of a coward to tell her that his own plan had failed.

Lilly waited. Night after night, she prayed for her chance to escape, but something kept her there, waiting. She could feel a purpose welling inside. Something was calling to her, readying her for her journey. Where it led, she did not yet know, but Lilly was certain she would be with her love again soon. Now the black mountains outside of her window did not look so bleak but filled her with hope and wonder.

CHAPTER 20

THE FOREST OF MANGÜ

All were in agreement that a trip to the forest of Mangü must take place, and soon. Frinz was to stay behind at the cottage with Mardra, and Zabrina would take Crystal and Brant on her mission. As they traveled, Brant and Crystal kept up an incessant string of chatter about anything and everything. Zabrina listened with amusement as they told of their childhood adventures. When they thought themselves unwatched, Crystal and Brant would speak softly and sweetly, sharing the secrets of their hearts.

They were well into the second day of their journey when Zabrina pointed to their destination far below. She landed at the edge of the forest and turned to them in quiet warning.

"We must enter here. If we were to fly above the place we are going, I fear that we might be unwelcome, so we will enter with caution."

They entered the forest, Zabrina leading the way, and moved quietly and quickly. The trees bowed, making way for the large dragon, and Crystal gasped at the sight. Brant laughed, amused that they were both still so surprised and excited by Thurnangl's magic.

The forest animals were much different from those they had encountered in the mountains near Mardra's home. Crystal found delight in chasing the colorful little lizards that buzzed through the air on iridescent wings. They darted back and forth before her, and she laughed.

Brant laughed with her. "Once," he told Zabrina, "when we were kids, she chased after a butterfly in the woods around our house and got lost. We were all so worried, and her parents and older siblings ran around in the forest, calling out her name. I found her in this small field in the middle of the forest, lying in the grass, just looking at the clouds. When she saw me, she smiled and whispered, 'This will be our secret place, just the two of us.'

"From that point on, whenever one of us was sad, or just felt lonely, we would both go there. We would pack a picnic basket and just sit there for hours. Everyone needs an escape from the rest of the world, and that was our spot. Although, I think we became an escape to each other."

Brant's face was a window to the love he held as he watched Crystal laughing nearby.

Zabrina smiled. "So, you have loved each other from the beginning, not even realizing it yourselves."

Brant's face turned red as he blinked in confusion, "B–but…I…we…but," he stammered.

Zabrina laughed, "Did you think a force as powerful as the love the Children of the Prophecy share would go unnoticed?"

Brant smiled. Her words were true. Thurnangl was different than where they had come from. There, the relationship they shared would be looked upon as foolish and short lived, but here their love was seen as an unbreakable connection.

Crystal ran to Brant with her hands cupped. She put her hands close to his face and opened them. Hidden there was a small, green puffball. At first glance, Brant thought she held a clump of moss, but looking closer, he saw tiny eyes staring up at him.

"Oh, wow! That's so cool!" Brant said, petting the little creature with his finger.

The puff let out a tiny peep, and Crystal squealed.

"Oh, it's so cute," Crystal said.

"Come," called Zabrina, moving forward, "we have much land to travel yet."

They walked on, amazed and awed by the various creatures peering from the forest trees. The day slipped away pleasantly, and the forest was soon growing dark. Using branches Crystal gathered, Brant lit a small fire. Zabrina settled in to sleep, leaving her charges to whisper and wonder at the sounds coming from the forest.

After a time, Crystal sighed heavily, "I can't sleep."

Brant, gazing at the tall trees above, rose from his sleeping place and held out his hand.

"Let's go," he invited.

She followed him, unquestioningly, as he began the climb up a large tree, towering high above.

They climbed higher and higher until their limbs tired. Then they rested, gazing out at the stars now visible from their perch. Crystal leaned into Brant, her head resting against his shoulder as she hummed a lovely tune. He wrapped his arms around her.

"I love you," Brant whispered.

Crystal chuckled, "Ah, but I love you more."

Brant laughed. Setting his head against Crystal's, he closed his eyes and fell asleep.

A loud squawk woke Crystal with a start. She opened her eyes to see a lizard, from her play the day before, sitting on her head, staring down at her. It squawked again, waking Brant.

"I guess it wants us to—," Crystal began.

The tree shook itself violently, and they were suddenly plummeting toward the ground, holding tightly to its trunk. The ground came closer and closer, the tree shrinking to the forest floor. Once there, it shook, dropping Crystal and Brant unceremoniously with a thud. Shivering slightly, it grew quickly to its original height.

"Ouch," Crystal said, rubbing her throbbing head.

"Whatever were you thinking?" growled an angry voice.

They looked up into the fierce and fiery eyes of Zabrina.

"We just climbed the tree," Brant said innocently.

"I was frantic! You must not leave without telling me. Had I not the power to speak with the trees and creatures of this forest, you would be lost to me."

Zabrina's look softened slightly. "But you are well, and so we must continue."

As they walked, they sensed Zabrina's anger subside.

"The village is not far from here. It will not be much longer now."

As if they had crossed an invisible line in the forest, everything changed. The air was still, and the creatures that had followed them scurried away. All was quiet.

"We have reached the outskirts of Kamzorves, the village of the Entremdor," Zabrina said in hushed tones.

Brant gave a small shiver as he looked about him. "Zabrina," he whispered uneasily, "why have we come to this place?"

"We seek their assistance in this war. We come to beseech Bahra, leader of the Entremdor to join our forces. From here, we will travel to the cave of Drinin."

They walked on, slowly and with unease. Zabrina pointed to the trees with her snout, and Brant and Crystal looked up to behold buildings wending through the branches of the forest above. They gasped in wonder at the homes peeking through the tree leaves, brilliant dots of color against the green of the forest canopy.

Their progress was halted by five guards waving spears menacingly. The sentinels stood tall—the height of two regular men—and their features were pointy and severe. Their bodies were covered in fine scales of deep purple that offset their glowing, yellow eyes. Sharp teeth gleamed in faces made unique by distinct and varied black markings.

"It seems that we have intruders in our village, Adair," snarled the center guard. He bore markings on his cheek in the shape of eyes.

"Tis true, Ulysses," replied the guard to the right. The markings on his face looked like wisps of smoke.

Stepping in front of her companions, Zabrina gave a low, menacing growl. "We come in peace to council with Bahra on behalf of Arron, Master of the Blades and leader of the armies of Thurnangl."

At her words, the guards lowered their weapons.

"This way," said Ulysses, bowing.

Crystal's eyes fell on the scaly tail unfurling behind him, and she nudged Brant. They moved toward the middle of the town, led by the guards. Shops lined the path, and Zabrina explained that only the homes of the Entremdor were built in the trees. Their business was conducted on the ground.

In the center of the village stood an enormous tree, thick as a building and reaching endlessly into the sky. They ascended, each using his or her own power and skill. The guards jumped effortlessly from the ground, instantly out of sight, while Zabrina motioned Crystal and Brant onto her back. Brant only smiled, and taking Crystal's hand, moved the earth below so that it elevated them swiftly.

Crystal, though enjoying the ride, rolled her eyes at Brant. "Show off."

As Crystal and Brant turned to enter the house, an Entremdor whispered to Zabrina, "I am very much impressed with their abilities. Not many of us believed that Crystal and Brant would come, let alone be so powerful."

Zabrina's response was chilly at best. "The Entremdor were vital in the Prophecy's creation. Your doubt does you no credit."

"There are many of us who are still faithful," he said, showing his sharp teeth as he smiled.

Two guards placed on either side of the entrance swiftly opened the blue door before Crystal and Brant. They stepped into an elegant room painted lavender. Tall windows were framed in sheer curtains that fluttered in the gentle breeze which lent its sweet perfume to the area. Rugs in beautiful pastels lay around the room, and a table slightly shorter than Brant's full height sat at the far end. Bahra, Ruler of Kamzoers, sat at the table, writing intently. She was a strikingly beautiful creature with eyes of the brightest pink glowing in a face marked with silvery vines. She smiled stunningly and beckoned them forth.

"Welcome, Zabrina and Children of the Prophecy. I hope all is well for you," Bahra's voice rang strong and beautiful through the room.

"Zabrina, Dragon of Healing, brings a message from Arron, now the leader of their army," a guard spoke, bowing.

"Their" army....I don't think they are going to help us, Brant thought.

Crystal could feel his uncertainty and whispered, "Don't worry, Zabrina knows what she's doing."

Brant nodded, hoping she was right.

Zabrina lifted her head proudly and spoke.

"Arron, Master of the Blades, calls the Entremdor to join the fight against Sörnam's forces. For the good of Thurnangl, he beseeches you."

There was a long silence. Brant felt a chill and shivered. He glanced at Crystal. From the look on her face she was uneasy as well.

Bahra sighed. "Why should your army require our help? I see no point in it. The last word we received from a....reliable source if you will, was that Arron led well and needed no assistance. Yes, I understand his heart aches with the loss of his father, but all the same, I do not intend to join in this war.

"We have kept to ourselves for so long, and I do not want my people used to serve the whim of selfishness. I know how battle works. In the last Great War, our people were used as puppets, no more than pawns to achieve selfish desires. I will not have my people used again. Some will say that those fighting on the other side of the war are evil and should be vanquished. Others protest that Arron's army seeks power for themselves. It matters not to me. There is nothing—"

"But," Brant began but hastily stopped himself.

"Well? Do you speak against me?" Bahra snapped, making Brant jump slightly.

Bahra rose from her desk. She walked briskly across the room and stared intently into Brant's eyes.

"Child, hundreds of years ago, when I was young, a dream came to me—a dream in which Thurnangl saved those driven from their homes, giving them a new hope. A war was soon to follow, plunging the land into chaos. I saw your faces bravely stepping forward to lead this land into prosperity and light, with unimaginable powers. The dream was so vivid and powerful, shaking me to my very core, I knew 'twas not a dream, but a premonition. My people kept it close, holding fast to the idea that, if it came to pass, then there would be a hope.

"As years passed, I helplessly watched my people succumb to a sickness which our magic could not cure. That very sickness spread, destroying this land beyond the trees and all those who stood on its soil. I did what I could to save the rest of my kind from falling to the same fate as so many of our brothers and sisters. We sealed away that which we could not take with us, and kept ourselves here. I watched my land, and my people perish once. I cannot bring myself to see that again."

Bahra looked away, her heart aching for so many loved ones she lost so long ago.

Brant stepped bravely forward. "You say we fight for selfish reasons, and that could be so, but what is more selfless than laying down your life for those you love? The people of Thurnangl do not fight for power or money. They fight to live. You of all people should know this. They fight for all who have died at the hands of the evil that spreads throughout the land.

"And do not think that sitting here, hidden away in the trees, will keep the evil from finding you. When it spreads, and it will, there will be no mercy for those who hid and did not fight. You ran away when your people were sick and dying, and rightfully. There was no choice then, but to run now, would be childish. Sörnam will destroy you and those you love, just as he destroys the people of Thurnangl. Will you sit here and call us selfish as we fight for those we love, or will you join us in protecting this land and its people?"

For a moment, Bahra sat in silence, and then a smiled stretched across her lips. She placed her hands on his shoulders, and kissed his forehead.

"That is very true. It seems you know just what it means to love someone."

Bahra glanced at Crystal. Seeing the Children of the Prophecy and the bond they shared, she could not hide the joy and comfort they gave her heart. She knew she must trust in the dream from so long ago.

"And you are right. We must protect what is precious in our forest and this land. Thank you for your brave, bold words, my child. I have made my decision. My people will aid you in this war."

Crystal's heart soared as she hugged Brant. "You did it!"

Zabrina nudged Brant. "Well done."

"I will send a message to Arron telling him of my response. You may stay here as long as you please." Bahra tuned and strode into another room dismissively.

A guard led them to their quarters.

"This is where you will stay," he said as he opened the door. It was just as large as the room they had left and bore the same decor.

Zabrina made herself comfortable on a rug in the corner and, with a final nod to her companions, closed her eyes.

"Brant, it seems our conversation in the forest holds true," she said with a final yawn.

Brant laughed as Crystal looked on in confusion. He smiled, pulling her close, and whispered, "I love you, Crystal."

Looking deep into his eyes, Crystal realized that it was silly to keep good and powerful feelings hidden. Hugging him tightly, she smiled.

"I love you too, Brant."

CHAPTER 21

DRININ

Brant woke early the next morning to find Crystal's bed empty. He sprang from his own, shaking the sleep from his head, and hurried to find her. He stopped as he heard the sound of singing in the distance. Following the song, he found himself at the window and stepped out into the canopy of thick tree branches.

When he found her, she was sitting on a nearby branch soaking in the early morning rays of sun. The light from the sunrise cast a glow that made her smile look more radiant than ever. He smiled as he listened to her sing the song she'd shared during Passing of the Shadows. From their place high above the ground, Brant could see nearby buildings and homes. Villagers had paused in their morning routine to listen to the beautiful girl and her lovely melody.

When the song had finished, Crystal looked at Brant and smiled. "Good Morning."

"Good morning!" he said, kissing her cheek.

She blushed, pleased. "I want to walk around town for a bit. Would you care to join me?"

"Gee, if I have to," he said teasingly.

Crystal stood and placed her hands on her hips. "Well you don't have to be so mean about it!" She turned her back to him.

"Hey, wait! I was just kidding!"

Crystal turned and stuck her tongue out before jumping into the nothingness below.

"What in the world is she doing?!" Brant said, searching below for any sign of her. He scrambled down until he spotted a boulder far below which he used as an elevator to reach the ground safely.

Crystal manipulated the air to slow her descent. She landed softly on the ground, cushioned enough to avoid injury. *Almost there, just a bit more,* she thought.

Brant landed next to her, and the rock turned to soft dirt.

He was about to scold Crystal, when a small voice cried, "Wow! That was Amazing!"

They looked down to see a small Entremdor child.

Crystal knelt and patted the youth's head. "Thank you. What's your name?"

The young girl bore markings on her faces that resembled little hearts.

"My name is Medina. I live in the tree across from Bahra. I am one of the few children here, and I heard you singing," she said looking at Crystal with sparkling eyes. "My mother said that you had a voice of gold!"

"That's very sweet of you, but really I'm not that good," Crystal said, slightly embarrassed.

An Entremdor woman approached and picked up Medina. Like the other Entremdor they had encountered, she was stunningly beautiful.

"I am sorry if Medina has been a bother," the female said in apology.

"No, no. Not at all," Crystal assured her. "She was only complimenting my song. It was very sweet of her."

"Yes," said the mother, "of the five children living in our village, she is the most open."

"There are only five children here? Why aren't there more?" Brant asked.

The Entremdor smiled as she explained, "Our people live to be of a great age, many to at least five hundred years. Our need for children is lessened by our lifespan, thus we have few and consider each one a rare blessing."

Crystal returned the woman's tender smile. "Yes we believe that where I come from too."

The mother hesitated before continuing, "Please, would you sing for us?"

Crystal blushed as she answered, "Well, I don't think that would be good I mean I don't —"

Crystal looked at Medina whose eyes sparkled at the thought of hearing Crystal sing once more. Taking a breath, Crystal began her song. The melody was beautiful and otherworldly. It flowed from her as though casting a spell. She let the song weave its melody, guiding her to its completion and finishing with a final trill. When she had finished, Crystal noticed more people had gathered to listen. The attention embarrassed her, but Crystal beamed and bowed at the deference they showed.

Zabrina found them there, surrounded by eager Entremdor. She sighed, her worry at their absence dissolving into amusement at the scene before her.

I wonder if Crystal will ever realize the true healing power of her voice. She knows so little of her own ability.

"My apologies for interrupting," Zabrina said, as the crowd parted for her, "but it is time for us to depart."

Crystal and Brant said goodbye to their new friends and prepared to set out. Their journey spanned most of the day, and it was nearing sundown when they spotted the great mountain ahead. It stood taller than anything they had seen before, and it towered above them as they made their way closer and closer.

Zabrina circled the mountain until she came upon the entrance to Drinin's cave. There she landed, and the group stood in silence, marveling at the vast cavern. Its entrance was large enough to dwarf even Zabrina's great form. Crystal shifted nervously, imaging how massive Drinin must be.

"Drinin?" Zabrina called.

They waited, listening to the echo of Zabrina's call through the cavern. Drinin lumbered forward, towering much taller than Zabrina but somehow less terrifying than Crystal expected. His scales were various shades of blue, like the ocean waves flickering in the sun.

"Yes? May I help you?" Drinin spoke only to Zabrina.

"Drinin," Zabrina began, "We come to ask you for your help in this war. Arron now leads the army, and he begs your support in the conflict to come."

Drinin sighed, "So Raymond has fallen, such a shame to lose a warrior as great as he. I do not doubt that the army will march well in Arron's hands, though he seems young."

"The young are more capable than you give them credit, Drinin," Zabrina said angrily, glancing at Crystal and Brant.

Drinin ignored her insinuation. "Nonetheless, I have no intention of helping the humans with such a war. The humans must be left to their own strength, to win or lose as they will. Their ranks have held these many years."

"But please—" Crystal said as he turned.

"I have no intention of letting a child tell me what to do," Drinin growled turning to face her.

He lowered his large head to hers. "For countless years, the Entremdor have taken the shape of the wizards and witches to walk this land, witnessing the destruction beyond this forest. Perpetuating war day after day, the people of this land fight and kill for the sake of greed and power. This civil war is a disgusting black and ugly thing that we refuse to be a part of."

"But," Crystal said, gaining courage, "if you do help, then you could end this. It's true. This war is a horrible thing that should never have begun, but there is more than just darkness here. There is light too. The people are drawn to the light. They want to finish this, for those they have lost and for those yet to come. We do not fight because we want to fight; we fight to bring the light to the people. We fight for freedom. Please, Drinin, will you fight with us?"

Crystal's words hung in the air as she stood, eyes locked with Drinin's, awaiting his answer.

Finally, Drinin smiled. "You are wise beyond your years, young one."

He turned to commend Zabrina. "They have been taught well."

The ancient dragon paused, in thought. "I will help you end this dreaded war."

Crystal hugged him before he could protest.

"Thank you, Drinin!"

It was agreed that, when the time came, Drinin would follow the Entremdor to Thurnangl. Arron's army was growing in power and strength, yet with every step forward the armies of Thurnangl took, so too did the evil of Phärnam.

CHAPTER 22

BLACK RAIN

Preparations continued and plans were carried out in the weeks following the visit with Drinin. The rainy season came to Thurnangl and they found themselves much indoors. On one such afternoon, Brant and Crystal sat with Mardra and Frinz, talking of their travels to the forest of Mangü and what awaited them in the days ahead.

"I'm gaining confidence in my healing," Crystal was saying, "and Zabrina tells me I have more healing power than I yet understand, but I feel like I've so far yet to go."

She paused a moment in thought. "I want to see if I can fly."

The room grew still as Crystal continued, "I know it sounds silly, but if I could just learn to focus the wind properly, I'm sure I could fly. I have to try."

Frinz smiled tenderly at Crystal. "Trust your powers, for only you know their true extent."

Thunder boomed outside, and Crystal flinched. "I really don't like storms."

Brant drew her close. "I'll protect you!"

Crystal blushed even as she moved closer, grinning.

Zabrina's eyes shifted to the entryway hall.

There was a sudden knocking at the door and Brant jumped to his feet. "Were you expecting anyone today?"

Frinz and Mardra shook their heads, confused.

Brant turned to the entryway, but Crystal ran past, eager to answer.

"I'll get it!"

Brant shrugged and sat back down.

As Crystal walked down the hall, the knock at the door became more insistent.

"Yes, I'm coming!" Crystal yanked at the door handle, eager to welcome their guests.

Any greeting she had planned died on her lips as she stared into the black eyes, dead and distant. She knew the woman before her without a second glance. Aaliyah had come, and with her a band of dangerous enemies. Crystal froze, her heart beating furiously.

Aaliyah smirked in satisfaction as she stared into Crystal's frightened face.

H-how in the world did they get here?! Crystal wondered. She blinked and regained her senses.

Barricading the entryway with a wall of thick ice, Crystal sprinted to warn the others.

"Problem! Aaliyah! Here with her guards!" was all Crystal could say before an explosion was heard and chaos ensued.

Mardra and the others ran to the hallway and found themselves severely outnumbered. Where, just minutes before, there had been ten soldiers to defeat; now there were thirty.

"Take the children, and kill the others!" Aaliyah barked.

Spells flew between them as Crystal and Brant's eyes locked. They turned and, as one, created a barrier of ice and steel to shield their friends from their enemies. Frinz, Mardra, and Zabrina would be safe. Using the air as a battering ram, Crystal forced Aaliyah and her gang from the house and followed them before securing the door.

Crystal and Brant stood together in the storm, surrounded by Sörnam's second-in-command and her forces. Aaliyah cast a lightning spell against a tree and watched as it fell toward Crystal. With a flick of her hand, Crystal blew the tree back to its upright position, freezing it in place with the rain pouring down upon them. She winked at Brant as she shot bullets of ice at their enemies.

Brant felt a loss in the lack of fire on this rainy night, but he used the earth around him to his advantage, taking out enemy forces with the sharp stones. The battle waged on and on, but Crystal and Brant were wearying. Their opponents were quickly overcoming them. Crystal glimpsed Brant fighting a crowd with his sword and knew what must be done. She knew she would break his heart, but she couldn't see him harmed.

Seizing her chance, Crystal ran to Brant's side and blasted all nearby attackers as far as she could, using her remaining strength to create an icy wall that would buy them a few more moments together and keep him from following. Brant blinked at the sudden silence as Crystal turned to him with tears in her eyes.

He shook his head as she whispered, "Brant, I love you."

Crystal launched herself into the air, propelling herself onto the towering wall of ice.

"Crystal?! What are you doing?!" Brant shouted.

She turned for a moment and smiled then disappeared on the other side.

Brant slammed rock after rock into Crystal's wall, but it would not break. The whipping wind made it impossible for him to levitate enough ground to create his own bridge over the wall. He could hear voices shouting from the other side, "Forget the boy! Grab the girl before she escapes!"

Silence followed. The rain grew heavier, and Brant saw nothing.

Brant stood in shock, unable to move forward, unable to think. As his world crashed around him, the steel wall in the cottage crumbled, and Frinz blasted through the remaining ice.

"Brant?! Crystal?!" she shouted, running to Brant.

One look at the enormous wall told her what had occurred. "Why? Why would she…?"

At her question, Brant revived and ran blindly down the wall. He searched for a way to shatter the ice before him. If he could break through, he could save her. His sword and his powers failed him, so he tried his fists—still nothing.

"Why?" he whispered.

Her voice came in his head. *Brant, I love you.*

He slammed his fists against the wall once more. "That's not good enough! We are in this together! You can't leave me! Come back to me….come back!"

Frinz, Mardra, and Zabrina looked on as Brant fought with the icy wall before them. They could not fathom what had occurred. Surely, Crystal could not have run away to fight alone. As their thoughts turned toward the fate that awaited Crystal should she be captured, hope dwindled.

"I pray that she will fight with all of the fire that burns within her heart—fight for her own life and for the lives depending on her," Mardra said looking in the direction Brant had run.

Crystal ran as fast as she could. She couldn't stop. She dared not stop; even to see if they were following. Mud weighed her down, and her breathing grew labored, but she would not stop until she knew Brant would be safe. The wall of ice continued to form beside her, and she let it dwindle. There was no need for it anymore. Brant had not followed.

Crystal's foot caught on a tree root, and she fell to the ground, scraping her head against a rock. She put a hand to her bleeding scalp and healed the wound. She was dazed and dizzy, but Crystal continued on. Time stopped, it seemed, as she ran on, and Crystal knew she must rest. Brant was safe, and her pursuers were not yet upon her. Taking advantage of a low-hanging tree branch, Crystal climbed to safety.

She could see her clear trail of deep footprints in the mud and muck, and Crystal knew that it would not be long until they would find her here, just as she wanted.

Aaliyah stalked into the clearing below, her soldiers following closely.

"She stopped here," Aaliyah said loudly.

"Should we split up, my lady?" asked a nearby witch.

"No, she's here and she will—,"

Crystal jumped out of the tree and landed in the middle of the group. Before they could move, she froze them into solid blocks of ice, which she blasted into the trees until they shattered. The remaining enemy was felled with shards of ice crafted from the falling rain.

It was over in second, and only Aaliyah and Crystal were left.

Aaliyah laughed menacingly. "That was very foolish of you. Nothing good will come of this for you."

Crystal clenched her fists, breathing heavily, "I don't care what happens to me. I will do everything in my power to make sure that I bring you down."

"How sweet. You honestly think you can win? You—a mere child?"

Aaliyah cast an illusion spell, and Crystal was suddenly surrounded by twenty replicas of the evil woman.

"You see, little girl. You are no match for my magic."

Crystal shot an ice shard through every version of Aaliyah, but they simply sliced through the illusions, leaving no mark.

Crystal looked around, her head spinning; she felt as if she was in a funhouse at a carnival. Aaliyah appeared behind Crystal, a spell on her lips. When Crystal turned and punched her squarely in the face, Aaliyah stumbled backward.

"Where I come from, that's how we fight," Crystal snarled.

Aaliyah stood, blood pouring from her mouth. Shocked and motionless, she screamed, "I am going to end this, here!"

Aaliyah stretched out her hand and recited an incantation so quickly, Crystal almost didn't hear it. Lightning burst forth, and Crystal's world plummeted into darkness.

Brant, leaning against the ice wall, felt it tremble. He opened his eyes and stepped away just as the wall collapsed in a river of water and mud.

Brant followed the muddy line where, moments ago, Crystal's ice wall had stood against him. The murky waters were the only clue of where his beloved might have gone. He walked on until a sharp pain sliced through his chest, bringing him to his knees.

This can't happen. We're supposed to be together always. I won't go back without her.

The pain remained, a white-hot knife, searing through his heart. He stood, immobile, fighting the thoughts that threatened to destroy him. Brant felt a hand on his shoulder, and his heart fluttered momentarily. He turned, a hint of hope in his eyes. Frinz stood before him, and the momentary light left his eyes.

"Brant, please, you have to go back. There is," her voice shook and tears ran down her face, "there is nothing you can do for her now. She is gone."

"NO!" Brant bellowed, and he pulled away from Frinz's well-meaning embrace.

"I won't," he said, his voice cracking with grief, "I can't believe that. I won't. I won't go back, not without her. If she's not by my side I just—"

Frinz touched Brant's face tenderly. "We know."

Brant could struggle no more. He let Frinz walk him to the house where the others waited in silent grief.

Frinz led Brant to his room where he sat staring blankly at Crystal's bed, still clean and tidy from the previous morning. He went to it and curled up where she would normally sleep, holding on to any hint of the girl he loved.

Brant's mind reeled with unspoken fears. Finally, closing his eyes against the pain, Brant slipped into a sea of unconsciousness.

CHAPTER 23
ENDLESS DARKNESS

Crystal thought she was dead; no, she was sure of it. But if she was dead, what were these voices breaking through her consciousness? Why was there dim light peeking in through the darkness? No, she could not be dead. Forcing herself to open her eyes, Crystal saw a vast room of cold, pale brick, from the ceiling hung Sörnam's banners.

Crystal blinked, bringing the rest of the room into focus. As she looked around, she recalled Frinz's words: "The people that are taken to Phärnam seldom return."

Crystal shivered where she lay. Aaliyah stood in front of a thrown, upon which sat Sörnam.

"You have succeeded. Excellent, Aaliyah." Sörnam's evil voice was little more than a hiss.

"Thank you, Master," Aaliyah said as she bowed.

This is bad. This is really, really bad. What was I thinking? Crystal thought. She made to rise, but a heavy foot pinned her to the cold floor.

"Oh, I see our prisoner is awake," Sörnam said with a sinister smile.

He rose from his thrown, a formidable figure in garments as black as pitch. As he sauntered toward her, his cape swished ominously behind him. He knelt close, the better to delight in her misery.

"It seems you have failed, my dear."

"I killed all of the others, didn't I?" Crystal spat in retort.

"Yes, yes, but they matter very little. They are nothing to you. You did a great thing, you know, running away as you did. You have bestowed on us a great gift. And yet, how will your friends bear your loss? Will they have the spirit to fight? Ha! I think not. The end of you will be the end of Thurnangl."

With a vicious laugh, Sörnam returned to his thrown. Crystal tried again to move, but the guard held her firmly with his foot. Gathering the air about her, Crystal blasted the guard in the face, freeing herself as he toppled over. She rushed toward Sörnam, fierce and ready to attack. Aaliyah restrained her, pulling her back violently by the hair, but not before the ice shard flew toward its target. Sörnam launched himself sideways, dodging the ice with an air of impatience. He signaled to his guards and smiled.

The guards bound Crystal's hands, then blindfolded and gagged her.

"Take her to the underground cell, and make sure she has no water," Crystal heard Sörnam say.

The guards pushed Crystal to move, but she struggled, intent on speaking her mind. Her words were nothing but muffled frustration.

"Keep moving," a guard barked as she was shoved forward.

Crystal was too weak to fight. Down an endless staircase they led her until she was sure they could go no further. They stopped finally, and Crystal heard the creaking of a heavy door. Her hands were unbound and the gag was removed from her mouth. Before she could scream, the blindfold was removed and she was pushed forward into the darkness. The door behind her slammed shut leaving her alone in the dark, cold cell.

With the darkness came the realization that Crystal was utterly alone. She was in the clutches of Sörnam, locked deep within his castle, and no one knew she was still alive. Brant was far away and had most likely given up any hope of her survival.

Even if hope remained, they knew she had been captured. They knew what awaited her in Sörnam's castle. She had let them down. She would never see Brant again, and she would die with the guilt of her failure weighing on her heart. Tears welled in Crystal's eyes, and she let them fall.

I have to try, Crystal thought. She pulled the water from her clothes, and freezing it into a pointed shard, blasted it at the door. The hole made by the shattering ice let light into her prison, and Crystal rushed toward the door. By the time she reached it, the door had repaired itself completely.

"This door is magic. You cannot just break through and escape. The room is enchanted as well. All water will be vaporized in mere seconds. Best not to waste what you have on fruitless escape attempts," said one of the guards outside.

Sure enough, Crystal looked to the floor, searching for her shards of ice, only to see them melted and vanishing with the enchantment's power. Crystal's heart sank. She pulled what little water remained from her clothes and gathered the droplets that had yet to evaporate from her precious ice shard. She tucked her collection into a small hole in the floor, praying the enchantment couldn't reach it in its frozen form.

Crystal looked around the dark room. Even as her eyes adjusted to the darkness, it was still difficult to see. The dry air parching her throat and skin weakened the end of Crystal's resolve. Collapsing to the floor she gave in to her hopelessness and tears. The hope was sucked from her being, and she sank to her knees with her face in her hands.

What have I done? I thought I could keep them safe…thought I could win…and instead I have failed them all. These people need the power Brant and I share to end this, and I've separated us. I'm such a fool.

Crystal lay on the floor, unable to move, for what seemed an eternity. She tried a few times to use the ring that linked her to Brant, but it brought her no solace. Whether the ring stayed silent because of the evil magic in Sürnam's castle or simply because her heart was breaking, Crystal couldn't tell. Brant felt farther away than ever.

Crystal, I love you. Brant's words echoed in her mind. Crystal balled her hands into tight fists, her resolve returning.

I have to keep going. I can't simply crumble. If I do, there really will be no hope. No matter what happens, I can't break here. I have to keep going. I got myself into this mess. I have to try to get myself out.

The quiet of the cell was crippling. Crystal did the one thing she could think of to ease her troubled soul—she sang. The sweet and simple notes calmed her, helping to regain her determination and strengthen her spirit. The melody echoed around her, even as the song ceased.

Crystal heard voices outside, and the door opened. Sürnam whisked into the room, bringing with him a heavy cloud of hatred.

Crystal sensed another power enter with him, something that went much deeper than just his presence. "You look quite cozy," he said in a voice of ice.

Crystal ignored him.

Sürnam frowned at his failure to provoke. "You will respond when I speak to you."

Again, Crystal remained silent.

Sürnam lashed out at her insolence, slapping her hard across the face. Crystal felt blood dripping from the gashes left by his long, sharp nails. Her only reaction was to smile.

"What reason do you have to smile!?" Sürnam screamed.

Crystal answered with disdain, "Here stands the great Sürnam, who let the presence of a mere child weaken his patience. You can't win, you know. At any cost necessary, I will stop you."

Sörnam glared at her in fury. "You say that now, but in due time, I am certain you will break. Your world will come crashing down until nothing matters anymore."

Smiling, he reached down and ripped the locket from her neck. "You will tell me everything. The pain, fear, and misery will become too great, and you will break. I'm sure of it….."

He leaned close and whispered, "Nothing matters anymore."

Sörnam turned and sauntered from the cell. Crystal sprang at him, but the door slammed before she reached him.

I have to… have to get it back…without my locket I can't—

"Please, stop! Give it back! Give it back!!!" Crystal shouted.

She banged her fists against the door, though she knew it would change nothing. Sörnam was already far away. Crystal sank to her knees, succumbing once more to the hopelessness of her condition.

"If you don't give it back, I can't heal." she sobbed.

Crystal had locked her healing powers into the locket, a physical item, instead of a memory or feeling. Zabrina had warned her of this very thing when she'd chosen the locket, but Crystal had been sure she would never take the locket off. Now, it was too late. All was lost.

Sörnam's words and very essence lingered in the room and consumed Crystal's mind.

It doesn't matter anymore.

Brant sat in front of the fire, moving little and saying nothing. He had remained so for two days.

"Is there anything we can do?" Mardra asked.

"No," sighed Frinz, "it is as I said. If she lives still, she has little chance of surviving. Brant feels it too. He knows she suffers. As she breaks, so too does he. There is little to be done until we know more."

Brant continued to gaze at the fire, the war in his head and heart raging silently on.

"I love you Brant! Everything is going to be just fine! Brant look at this! Brant, it doesn't matter anymore."

Brant looked up from the fire. All eyes were on him now, waiting for some sign of hope.

"It doesn't matter anymore," Brant said in a low voice. "Nothing can come of this, because it doesn't matter anymore."

Frinz's eyes welled with tears. "Please, Brant, do not say such things. Crystal is strong. Please do not lose hope!"

"But that's what she said," Brant replied. "It doesn't matter anymore."

Frinz buried her face in her hands, defeated. "This cannot be. We must not fail. I know not what more to do!"

Mardra clasped her daughter's hand. "Take heart, Frinz. We must seek out Liane. She may have the answers we desire. I shall go. You must not leave Brant."

Frinz was overcome by her mother's words and the renewed hope they brought. Her gratitude went unspoken, but her eyes met Mardra's, and she nodded. Perhaps, hope remained after all.

CHAPTER 24
THE FIGHT TO SURVIVE

Once her tears began, Crystal could find no will to stop them. She felt herself slipping away, and she knew that Brant could feel it too. Helpless and hopeless, she let the dark thoughts flow. *Everything is over now. There is nothing left but pain. Please, just end it.*

Entrenched in despair, Crystal hardly noticed Sörnam's return. He grasped her chin and looked into Crystal's eyes. Their rich blue was beginning to fade into pitch black.

"Our work is going well," Sörnam hissed. "Your mind is almost mine. This curse has taken a strong hold upon you. Time and time again, I have used it on those I have captured, and not a one has escaped its grasp. It will eat away at your resolve, and then your soul. This curse is strong indeed, and with my power, it is unstoppable. None will stand in its way, and that includes you."

The evil surrounding Sörnam was palpable, and Crystal heard it call to her.

"Nothing matters anymore."

Crystal felt Sörnam's power tearing at her soul, crushing the link between her heart and Brant's. She could no longer fight and bowed her head wordlessly.

Sörnam barked a laugh of pure hatred. "What a difference a day has made. Look at you now."

He leaned closer. "Tell me where the Stone of Power lies."

"I…"

Though Crystal's spirit was broken, she could not betray the secret her friends were fighting so hard to preserve.

"The Stone of Power," she whispered slowly, "does not belong to you."

Sörnam's eyes widened, and he roared, "We shall see about that!"

Grabbing her hair, he yanked her head back until she was staring into his enraged face.

Crystal winced. "It doesn't matter. It's just like you said. I don't care what happens to me. Kill me if you wish," her body shook violently, "but I will never tell you where the Stone of Power is hidden."

"Then I will take the information I need!"

Sörnam began to chant. Suddenly, Crystal could feel him invading her mind, taking her memories.

"NO!" Crystal screamed.

She used all of the power she could find within her, painfully ripped her mind from his grasp. She shoved him as hard as she could and Sörnam fell back, hitting the wall.

"How dare you!" Sörnam spat, casting a spell. "Frectore!"

Crystal screamed as pain seared through her body. The very blood that ran through her veins boiled, scorching her insides. She wished for the end, for death, but the spell stopped with the snap of Sörnam's fingers.

He sneered viciously, "Good, but perhaps not enough. Let us try another tactic." He dangled her locket before her and whispered, "Acontr."

Crystal felt as though her lungs were filled with liquid and ice. She could neither breathe nor fight. Coldness, like nothing she had ever felt, seeped through her, freezing her very core. She looked up to see her locked glowing red in Sörnam's grasp. Crystal could neither speak nor scream.

"Ah, I have silenced the songbird. I shall come back soon to finish you," Sörnam whispered with contempt. "When we meet again, you will tell me where the Stone of Power is, and I promise to end you quickly."

He strode to the door, laughing.

Crystal raged silently, her screams unheard and unfruitful. *It doesn't matter anymore.*

Crystal slipped into unconsciousness, dreaming of Brant. They were running in the forest near the cottage.

Brant was teasing, "Crystal, I bet you can't catch me!"

Crystal laughed and ran after him. "Hey! Slow down!"

Brant kept running as she followed. He didn't turn around.

"Brant! Wait up!" Crystal said.

On and on they ran, Brant always just out of her reach.

"Brant! Wait up!" she called nervously.

The game was no longer fun, and she reached out to grab his hand but found herself rooted to the ground, watching as Brant ran on. She tried calling to him, but her screams were muted. She watched him run away from her into the darkness.

She awoke, weeping, and drew into herself with grief.

Brant, please, please come back, she thought. She couldn't even whisper his name into the darkness.

She heard the door to her cell opened, but Crystal cared little. She was completely broken.

Please, she thought, *just end this. I can't take this pain anymore.*

Sensing a light in the darkness, Crystal opened her eyes. In the glow of candlelight, she spied a young woman with eyes like pink cherry blossoms studying her kindly. She sat next to Crystal and took the frightened child's hand.

Am I still dreaming? Crystal thought.

The woman spoke in a sweet, soothing voice, "You need not fear me. My name is Lilly, and I have come to help. My brother has taken much. Let me help you get it back."

Crystal's eyes widened. *Brother? How can she bare any relation to that monster?*

Lilly patted her hand comfortingly. "I understand this must confuse you greatly. I am younger sister to the evil man who holds you, but we are nothing alike. I come in secret to free you. I have spent years held captive in this evil place, and it has become my work to know every corridor and corner. I have attempted to use them to free myself and those who were captured before. Sadly, I was too late for the other poor souls."

Crystal looked down and shook her head. *It doesn't matter anymore. I'm too weak and powerless. Everything is gone—my voice, my heart, my love.*

Lilly took Crystal's face in her hands, looking deep into her eyes. "His curse has taken hold of you more powerfully than I thought possible."

Lilly studied Crystal in silence for a great while.

"I know how you must feel. I too am trapped, kept from the people I love, kept from the one who holds my heart. But you must cling tightly to your love and to those who await your return. Fight for them, Crystal. You must fight!"

Crystal bowed her head and nodded.

"All will be well. Take this for your comfort." Lilly handed Crystal a water jug and small pack with dried fruit and nuts. Crystal clung to the water jug tightly as Lilly continued. "Your will is strong. You must fight the curse so that you may escape. Your love awaits you."

Crystal ate and drank, regaining her strength of body and heart. Lilly made to depart through a hidden passage under the floor, but Crystal grabbed her in desperation. She tried to speak to her new friend, but the words would not come. Sighing, she pointed to the door and to Lilly, who waited anxiously.

"You wish me to go with you?" Lilly asked blinking.

Crystal nodded, a small smile touching her lips.

Lilly considered Crystal's request, feeling as though a piece of her destiny was falling into place.

"With you as a distraction, we may just succeed, but for now, take this." She tucked a note into Crystal's hands. "Give this to Frinz. I believe it is vital to success in this war."

A guard stirred in his sleep as Lilly's incantation of slumber beginning to dissipate.

Lilly kissed Crystal on the forehead and whispered, "We shall meet by the winged rock near the river. Let your heart guide you, and worry not for me, dear Crystal. The people of Thurnangl depend upon you."

With that, Lilly was gone. Crystal hid the note in the remains of her food pack and squared her shoulders, letting hope peek through the darkness.

I will not despair, but hope. The people need hope, and that dies here with me, unless I fight. I will escape. I will find Brant, and no evil will stop me.

CHAPTER 25

DEAF

Mardra returned in the early hours of the morning with Liane. They had travelled through the night, relying on Zabrina's strong wings to bring them to Brant before all was lost. Liane wasted no time in seeing to Brant. With a nod at Frinz, she sat next to the despondent boy. Her brow creased with worry as she put her hand to his forehead.

"Frinz, would you please take out the white leaves from this basket and boil them for me?" Liane asked.

Frinz did not move from her spot on the rug.

"It is alright. I will do it," Mardra said.

"No. She must do it. Please, Frinz, will you boil these leaves for me?"

When her friend gave no response, Liane hugged Frinz fiercely.

"This is not your fault, my friend. We must not let our fear keep us from saving Crystal. We must help Brant. He depends on you. They both do. Please."

Frinz started, as if shaken from a dream, and began the task of boiling the leaves. As the room filled with their soft scent, Frinz felt herself relax.

"What a lovely smell."

"Yes, they are meant to relax the body and soothe the mind," Liane said looking to Brant, but he remained unchanged.

She stared deep into his eyes, watching as the vibrant green, slowly turned to black. His eyes stared blankly ahead, devoid of happiness.

"Brant, you must be strong. You must fight the hopelessness in your heart. Crystal would not want this for you, would she?"

Brant blinked and stared at the fire, tears spilling from his eyes. "It doesn't matter anymore. That's what she said. There's nothing I can do."

Liane frowned. "This is no good. He is lost to us."

She looked into the worried faces of her companions and continued, "He has heard Crystal fall into despair, and it has broken him. He hears nothing from her now and will hear nothing further from us. The tie is shattered, and Crystal has given up hope."

"But that just cannot be! Crystal would never lose hope ever!" Zabrina argued.

"I speak only the truth I sense." Liane sighed. "It looks as though Crystal is close to death."

The room grew suddenly still.

"We could rally a rescue team and travel to Phärnam," Mardra suggested. "We could save her."

"It will not work. No one has ever breached the defenses of Phärnam. We cannot risk the lives of many to save one who might already be lost," Frinz said, her voice cold and resigned

Liane clasped Frinz's hand tightly.

"We must wait and hope that Brant finds his way back to us. I do not see any other way," Liane said.

"And so we wait," Zabrina concurred.

They watched the shadows stretch across Brant's face.

Brant did not sleep again that night but slipped into an unconsciousness filled with nightmares, unable to escape the voices that called to him in agony. Suddenly, one clear voice rose above the noise in his mind.

"Brant, I love you!"

Brant saw her as he heard the words and made his way toward Crystal, but she smiled and turned away.

"Crystal! Come Back! Please!" Brant ran toward her but could not catch her fleeing form. For hours he ran, but still she alluded him.

"CRYSTAL!" he screamed in agony.

Brant woke from his terror suddenly. He lay in her bed, but she was gone. Burying his face in her pillow, Brant gave in to his despair and sobbed.

Crystal listened to Sürnam's approaching footsteps and quickly swallowed the food, stowing the rest. She sat against the wall, the water jug and pack behind her. Crystal's heart pounded as she willed herself calm.

Sürnam walked through the door and knelt before Crystal, her locket dangling from his wrist. Crystal felt the heaviness of evil surround her as it had before. It consumed her mind and body, paralyzing her, but this time she was stronger. This time she could fight.

"Now," Sürnam whispered. His icy breath felt cold against the top of Crystal's head. "Let's see if we can see where the Stone of Power is today."

Sürnam reached for her, and Crystal smiled. With a flick of her hand he was thrown across the room, the water from the jug pinning him there. Before the guards could react, Crystal had frozen their legs, leaving them immobile.

Sürnam rose to his feet as Crystal dashed through the doorway. "You will pay for this!" Sürnam spat.

With a grin of triumph, Crystal shot a dart of ice through the evil lord's sleeve, nailing it to the wall. She fashioned a whip and used it to extract her locket from Sörnam's grasp. Placing the chain around her neck, Crystal felt the evil grip of Sörnam's spell release her completely.

"See ya!"

With a quick wave, Crystal was up the stairs and out of Sörnam's sights.

She used every ounce of strength to escape. She could feel Sörnam's wrath following her through the corridor

Sörnam's voice rang from all around her as though he was talking through an intercom.

"Crystal has escaped! Catch her at once, and you will be rewarded!"

At the top of the stairs, Crystal was met by five guards. She quickly dispatched them with a gust of wind and ran straight toward the window at the end of the hall. Suddenly, she was blown forward, the air knocked from her lungs. Sörnam stood at the top of the stairwell, a look of contempt darkening his features.

"You are altogether too bold for my taste, child."

Crystal fought the urge to cower on the floor and stood to face her pursuers. She unleashed an onslaught of icy knives at the group. The first one missed its mark, but the second sliced Sörnam from lip to brow. The blood that pooled in the wound was black as night. As it oozed across his cheek, his guard's gasped in horror. Sörnam bore the mark of ultimate evil—black blood.

Crystal blinked, coming to grips with the scene before her. Guards were whispering and inching further from their master. With a final look at her captor, Crystal turned to the window.

"Serves you right," were her last words as she sprang to freedom.

"You fools! Stop her!!" Sörnam ordered his guards.

Crystal used air to make herself glide down to the outside of the castle. She stood on the outer wall and looked back. She smiled, jumped down, and started to run as fast as she could. Her heart was still pounding as she ran. Her breath was fast and shallow, but she didn't stop. She did not want to stop.

Time seemed to move so fast, it seemed like she had only been running for a few minutes when she came to the river. When she turned around, she was relieved to find no one had followed her. She did not see the rock with wings. Crystal looked around, but it was still dark and the rain was hard to see through. After walking through the slippery mud and tumbling a few times, Crystal saw the rock close to the water's edge. Sitting on the rock was Lilly.

"Lilly!" Crystal shouted, running toward her.

Lilly smiled with relief. "You have escaped. All is well!" She embraced her new friend tightly.

"Yes," laughed Crystal, "thanks to you! Where will you go now?"

Lilly gave a tender smile, "I shall seek out my love, the one who holds my heart!"

Crystal's heart leapt. "Me too. I hope you get there safely."

"You as well, my dear. Go with great haste, for he needs you," Lilly said.

She kissed Crystal gently on the forehead and departed. Crystal watched Lilly until she could see her friend no more. With a smile, she turned in the direction her heart lead. She turned toward Brant, toward home.

CHAPTER 26
RACE AGAINST TIME

On and on, Crystal ran as the night grew darker around her. The wind and rain came at her from every side, and lightning flashed above. She willed herself to continue on, knowing that every step was one closer to Brant. She continued until she could go no further and then sought shelter in a hollow tree. Curling up under its meager protection, Crystal drew the water from her soaked person. Exhausted from all she had endured, her eyes began to close and she was soon lost in dreams.

"Bet you can't catch me!" Brant called as he turned and started to run.

Deep in her mind, Crystal felt a pang of familiarity. Had she been here before?

"Hey! Wait for me!" she shouted.

Brant didn't turn around as she chased after him.

She laughed, "Brant, wait up!"

She reached for his hand, but suddenly her feet stayed rooted in place.

"Brant! Wait, don't go! Brant!!" Crystal called after him, but he didn't turn around. He kept running and disappeared into the darkness.

Crystal sank to her knees.

"What if I don't make it? What if I'm too late? Why was I so stupid? Brant, I'm sorry. I'm trying as hard as I can to reach you. Please don't leave me here all alone!"

Crystal paused for a moment then whispered, "I want to be with you."

She awoke to a crack of thunder, her dream all too real. Brant wasn't with her. It was dark and raining, and Crystal was alone. She wept.

I can't do this, not now! I have to keep going. I have to see him! Why do I feel like something is dragging me down and slowing my heart?

A sudden and terrifying realization hit Crystal— Sörnam's curse. She had fled, escaped his grasp, but the curse still bound her very heart and soul, the very heart and soul tied to Brant. The curse had reached through Brant and taken a deep hold upon him, even while she eluded part of it, another lingered. She knew without a shadow of a doubt that the only she could escape this vile curse and restore Brant's strength was to reach him, and she must reach him before the curse took its toll.

She must move forward, even if it killed her. She would fight her way back to Brant's side and see him once more. She prepared to leave her shelter in the tree, but the arrival of a tiny creature in her lap stopped her. She blinked through the darkness at the shivering ball of fur, trying to determine what it might be.

A flash of lightning revealed a round, fuzzy animal, slightly bigger than her hand. Oversized ears rested atop its head, and tiny spikes jettisoned from the end of its tail. It gazed at her with large, intense eyes. Its four tiny legs were curled under it for warmth.

How cute, she thought, stroking the animal and pulling the water from its wet fur.

"See, little one, everything is ok now. There's nothing to fear. It's just rain," Crystal soothed.

She stopped suddenly. These were the very words Brant often spoke to her, and now she prayed that they would be true.

The animal looked up as a flash of lightning lit its face, shining in its umber eyes.

"You're Crystal," it squeaked, its voice high and soft.

Crystal blinked. *It-it spoke?*

"Greetings, Crystal! Whiticker is happy to meet thee. Whiticker has been so alone these past months, for Whiticker is the last of the Nezando."

"I'm so sorry," Crystal said.

"It is alright. Whiticker knows his family is watching over him, and that fills Whiticker with joy!" the little creature said contentedly.

As the thunder boomed, Whiticker jumped to Crystal's shoulder in fright, burying himself in her hair.

"Whiticker does not care for the rainy season," he whispered. "Last year was Whiticker's first rainy season, a terrible time. But Crystal can make the rain stop, yes?"

Crystal held Whiticker in her arms, and laughed.

"Well yes. In truth, I can, but I don't want to take away the water needed by the trees and animals and water creatures."

There was another loud crack of thunder outside. Whiticker jumped, and Crystal giggled.

"Well, I guess I could make it slow down just a little."

Whiticker relaxed in Crystal's arms.

"Then can Crystal sing to Whiticker, like mama used to do?"

Crystal nodded and began to sing. Her soothing voice filled the air around them. The song, slow and beautiful, calmed all of the animals. The storm lightened but the rain did not stop. Her gentle voice rang through the trees, and the sweet sound lulled Whiticker to sleep. Tucking him safely in her arms, Crystal moved from her hiding place and continued her journey. The final notes of her song lingered about them as she ran.

The rain grew heavier after a bit, but all remained quiet. As morning grew near, the sky lightened, and Crystal could see the path ahead. Whiticker woke well into their journey. He blinked and listened for the thunder and lightning, but there was none.

He looked up at Crystal and beamed.

"Wow! Crystal really made the loud booms and cracks stop! The stories momma told Whiticker are true! Thank you, Mama!"

Giggling, Whiticker jumped from Crystal's arms and skipped along beside her.

"What stories?" Crystal asked.

"Whiticker remembers Mama telling him stories of the Children of the Prophecy. All of the creatures of Thurnangl know about you. We are all part of this war. Whiticker's family proved that."

Whiticker looked sad for a moment.

"It sounds like you love your family very much," Crystal said.

"Yes! Whiticker could tell many stories of Mama and Papa and everyone for a long time! Whiticker has an idea!" Whiticker skipped ahead of Crystal and looked back at her. "Whiticker will tell you lots of stories.....but before Whiticker tells you he has one question. Why is Crystal alone? Where is Brant? The stories that mama told Whiticker said that the Children of the Prophecy are together always."

Crystal slowed her pace to a walk, and looked at the ring on her hand.

"Well," Crystal said, "I'm alone because some of Sörnam's people came, and I ran away to lead them away from Brant and our friends, but I didn't win the fight. I was taken to Sürnam's castle and for a while I lost hope. I didn't think I was going to live, and I didn't want to.

"Someone very kind helped me escape from the castle, and that's how I got out. So now I have to get back to Brant. When he and I are apart, it feels like my heart is being torn apart. I have a feeling that's it's because we've both been traumatized and," Crystal paused to take a breath, "I am afraid Brant thinks I'm dead. I think that everyone has lost hope that I will return. Everything is my fault. Why can't I just keep it together?"

Crystal put her face in her hands. "I'm just so pathetic!"

"Please," Whiticker said, walking closer, "Please do not be sad, Crystal. Whiticker will help you get to Brant. He knows where you were hiding. He knows of the burnt down magic house. He has seen it before. Whiticker will help you, so you can smile again."

"But even if I do, what if Brant isn't ok, all because of me? We're both so hurt, and it's all my fault."

Whiticker looked at Crystal.

"It is not your fault. You did what you thought was best. You were trying to protect Brant and everyone else. Once Brant sees that you are alive, he will be very happy."

Crystal looked at Whiticker and wiped the tears off her face. "Yes I have to do my best, no matter what. Thank you, Whiticker."

They continued to run for the rest of the day, stopping only to eat and rest briefly, until it was too dark to see.

They found a small cave to stay in for the night. Crystal rested her head on the bag Lilly had given her and looked at the roof of the cave. Whiticker lay on her stomach, rising and falling with every breath she took.

"So, Whiticker?" Crystal asked.

Wagging his tiny tail, Whiticker lifted his head.

"How come you're so nice to me? You're helping me find my way back, and I didn't do anything for you."

Whiticker laughed. "Crystal was kind to Whiticker first. She made Whiticker feel better when the storm was angry. And…" Whiticker paused, "and Crystal is Crystal. She and Brant are the ones who will bring an end to this war, and the sooner the war ends, the sooner the bad people will go away. The bad people…..are the reason Whiticker was all alone for so long. They dug up our homes. We lived in burrows, but they dug up the trees and the ground so they could use them. It was just Whiticker and mama in the burrow. Papa died just before Whiticker was born. Mama told me that Papa went with one of the people who had special powers, and he fought in the war."

Crystal sat up, and Whiticker continued. "Mama said he was very brave and gave his life for ours, but they dug up our home and killed all of my friends and neighbors. Mama took Whiticker far, far away, where no one would find us. Someone saw mama.

"Mama jumped into a bush and hid Whiticker in it. She kissed Whiticker and said, 'I love you,' then she jumped. It was really quiet. The only sound was a whisper of a spell, and I never saw mama again."

Whiticker buried his face in Crystal's shirt. "But Mama and Papa are together, right? They're together and they're happy. Because they're watching over me in that beautiful place in the clouds. And they're happy while watching over me, yes?"

Crystal hugged Whiticker tightly as he cried.

"I'm sure that right now they're watching over you, and they're very proud of you. I'm sure of it."

Whiticker looked earnestly at Crystal.

"Please, Crystal, is it ok for Whiticker to stay here with you where he is not so lonely?"

Crystal smiled and petted his little head, "Of course you can, Whiticker. I will take care of you. I promise."

Crystal sang Whiticker to sleep. She stayed awake for a while. She did not want to go to sleep for fear of losing herself in nightmares again. She knows that, with every dream she had, Brant was trapped deeper in his own nightmares. Brant was slowly dying, and his pain was taking Crystal with it.

Finally, she could fight it no longer, Crystal's eyes grew heavy and she fell asleep. This dream was different. She could hear Brant calling her name as he stood in the doorway of Frinz's house. He beckoned her to follow and went inside. She beamed, she was so close now.

"Brant!" Crystal called out.

She ran as fast as she could, but she never moved closer to the house and to Brant. It was always the same distance away, and the door was still open. Rain began to fall, and the ground turned to mud.

"Crystal, please. Please help me," Brant whispered.

His voice was pure anguish, and it wrenched at Crystal's heart. She tried to run faster, but she never got closer. Suddenly, her feet wouldn't move. She looked down to see that the mud was growing thicker, and she was sinking.

"Brant! Please don't give up! Hold on!!!" Crystal cried.

"Crystal," Brant's voice faded away as Crystal's head sank below the mud.

Crystal awoke with a start. She gasped for air as though she really had been underneath thick mud. Her body trembled as she tried to control her breathing.

"Crystal? Are you ok?" Whiticker asked worriedly.

"Yes, I'm fine, but I need to get to Brant. If I don't hurry, he won't survive."

Brant was asleep. In his dream, he was running through the forest. He could hear Crystal calling out to him, and he looked everywhere. There was no sign of her, but he could hear her voice. The rain was heavy, and the earth was muddy.

Brant sank to his knees and held his head.

"Please make it all stop. I can't take it anymore. I just want it to end. This world means nothing without her. She's gone."

A crack of lightning woke Brant. He saw the enchanted ceiling with the ocean water washing over the beach.

It doesn't matter anymore.

He knew his heart was close to its breaking point. It wouldn't be long before it all ended. He hoped it would be quick so that he could be with Crystal.

Crystal and Whiticker traveled as fast as they could. They were silent most of the way, trying to keep their pace.

"We're almost there, Crystal!" Whiticker shouted over the loud rain.

Almost there I just have to— Crystal gasped.

It felt as though a blot of white hot lightning shot through her heart. She stopped and fell to one knee.

"Crystal? Crystal! Are you alright?" Whiticker asked, resting his paw on her knee.

Crystal gripped her chest. Her heart was beating violently, and she grew dizzy.

"We're r-running out of time," she choked.

Crystal rose to her feet and took a few wobbly steps forward.

Please, Brant. You can't give up. I'm so close now! Please, hold on.

Crystal put one foot in front of the next, willing herself forward through the pain.

Crystal, I love you.

She forced herself forward. It mattered not that it hurt to move. She must keep going.

"Crystal, stop!" Whiticker said.

Crystal paused and looked down at Whiticker, just steps from the edge of a cliff. A bolt of lightning brightened the sky, and Crystal could see, below her in the trees, the outline of Mardra's house. Tears of relief filled her eyes.

He's right there.

Crystal screamed, as loud as she possibly could, "BRANT!" Her voice echoed through the trees.

Brant sat up and blinked as Crystal's voice called to him. He rose slowly from bed and made his way downstairs and toward the door that would lead him outside. Frinz, Mardra, and Zabrina looked worriedly as he passed through the kitchen.

"Brant?" Frinz asked, concern etched on her face.

He made no reply and continued toward the front door. Opening it, he walked outside and into the rain.

Frinz rose from her seat to follow him, but Liane put a hand on her shoulder.

"Let him be. Maybe this is what he needs."

Crystal looked down at Whiticker and smiled. He looked over the edge of the cliff, but he could not see the bottom.

The ground beneath Whiticker crumbled suddenly, and Crystal saw him fall into the darkness below. She wasted no time but jumped after him, catching him and holding his little form close as they fell together. The wind whipped and roared around them. And then they were soaring, not sinking. Crystal mastered the wind about her and used it to glide gracefully over the treetops.

Whiticker opened his eyes, and his fright turned to wonder.

"Crystal! You can fly!"

Crystal could only laugh. The second her feet hit the ground, she began to run. Whiticker and Crystal were caked in mud and soaked in rain, but neither of them cared. Crystal was so close now.

Brant stood alone, the only sound the rain pouring down around him. Crystal's voice still rang in his ears. He had heard her. He knew it, somehow. He looked to the night sky, watching the rain fall in sheets. He closed his eyes.

"BRANT!"

He opened his eyes and looked about, seeing nothing but darkness. *A dream,* he thought, and then he blinked. Through the trees he saw something come, coming to him. *Crystal.*

Crystal squinted through the darkness until she saw him standing there, looking at the rain. "BRANT!" she called and sprinted forward.

Brant looked out and saw Crystal.

A dream, he thought, but as she got closer and closer, he blinked. *No it's not a dream Crystal is alive? Crystal, Crystal—*

"CRYSTAL!" Brant ran forward, and Crystal leapt into his arms. Brant held her tightly so neither of them would fall, burying himself in her embrace. They stood there for a moment, holding tight to one another. Brant brushed the hair from Crystal's face and kissed her.

"I thought you were dead! I didn't even—I wasn't—I love you!"

Crystal laid her head against Brant's chest.

"I love you too. I'm so sorry. I never should haven—,"

Brant silenced her with a kiss. "It doesn't matter anymore. We're together."

Crystal beamed. "Let's promise here and now that we'll be together forever, ok?"

"I promise. We'll be together always."

Whiticker laughed, and Brant looked down at him.

"Who is this?" he asked.

"This is Whiticker. He helped me find you." she explained.

Whiticker jumped into Brant's arms and squeaked, "It is nice to finally meet you, Brant!"

Brant smiled and led Crystal into the house, grasping her hand as though he would never let go. Crystal walked into the kitchen to the shocked faces of her friends.

Her eyes shone with emotion as she smiled and whispered, "I'm home."

At the site of Crystal alive and well, her friends leapt from their seats in joy, hugging the weary, rain-soaked girl. Amidst the tears and exclamations, Crystal sighed and sank into a chair, relieved to have made it home. Brant started at the sight of her face in the light.

"What happened to you?" he asked, his fingers tracing the three, deep scratches on her cheek.

In her weakened state, she'd been unable to heal them before they left their permanent mark. Crystal yawned in utter exhaustion.

"Is it ok if I tell you in the morning? I'm just so tired, I could fall over."

Frinz smiled and kissed Crystal's head.

"From all you have been through, I would expect nothing else, rest well."

Crystal and Brant walked up the stairs, hand in hand, Whiticker trailing behind. She changed into fresh clothes quickly, collapsed into bed, and was asleep within seconds. Brant smiled and sat on her bed, stroking her hair, and watching her sleep peacefully.

"You love each other very much, do you not?" Whiticker asked gently

Brant smiled and kissed Crystal's forehead. She smiled in her sleep, still dreaming, finally safe.

"Yes, Whiticker. Very, very much."

When Crystal awoke late the next morning, everyone was downstairs waiting for her. Whiticker was sleeping next to her on her pillow. Crystal sat up, rubbing her eyes as she stretched. Whiticker woke and jumped into Crystal's lap.

"Did you sleep well?"

"Very much so!" Crystal laughed as she moved to dress.

She chose a pretty dress, the color of a summer sky, to match her renewed happiness. Making her way downstairs, she heard the others cease talking as she approached.

"Good Morning," she said to them.

She settled into the open seat that awaited her. After a few moments of silence, Crystal took a deep breath and began her story. She told them of all that had happened, pausing only when she reached the part in her story where Lilly appeared. Remembering the note she carried, Crystal ran upstairs to fetch it. She handed the message to Frinz and finished her tale.

"This is for you, from Lilly," Crystal said.

Frinz took the folded piece of paper and read it. Her eyes widened and she looked from Crystal to Brant.

"Well, this certainly is unexpected...I—this is—I—," Frinz stumbled over her words and she returned the note.

Crystal held the note as they both read it. Its contents gave them pause, and they locked eyes in amazement.

"I have a good feeling about this," Brant said with a smile.

"Me too," Crystal replied.

Liane was next to read the note and smiled her approval. "Yes. This is the right course."

Brant and Crystal were suddenly seized by a united urge deep within, as if something were calling to them alone. They squeezed hands but were compelled to stay silent. They could not explain their feeling or the need to keep quiet, but they knew without speaking that something beckoned them forth. The end of this war was coming, and their purpose was almost upon them.

Suddenly, there was a knock at the door, and the group froze.

CHAPTER 27

ANGERWIN'S DEAL

Angerwin, Dragon of Fire, stepped quietly into Sörnam's thrown room.

Sunlight danced across her scarlet scales, casting magnificent dancing rubies onto the surrounding walls. Sörnam sat on his thrown, wounded and fuming.

He had lost Crystal, and Lilly had escaped amid the chaos. In the struggle, he'd been left with a deep gash across his face and no healer to cure it. A bandage, black with his blood, lay plastered to the wound, doing little to comfort him. The castle was abuzz with talk of the horrors his guards had witnessed. Sörnam took morbid delight in the fear now renewed in his subjects. He needed only their fear to control them.

Sörnam glanced at Angerwin in disgust. "What do you want, you vile creature?" he spat.

"I have a deal for you, Sörnam," Angerwin growled.

Narrowing his eyes, Sörnam leaned dangerously close. "What deal could tempt me?" Angerwin bared her teeth and produced a piece of parchment. "I have in my possession a map of Thurnangl which reveals the location of the Stone of Power."

Sörnam leapt from his thrown and snatched the paper. Examining it, he found that it was blank.

"What?! Where is it?! Tell ME!"

Angerwin glared, smoke pouring from her snout.

"I have hidden the true map. You shall have it when we strike our deal."

Sörnam hissed in rage as he regained his thrown.

"Very well. You have my attention."

Angerwin hesitated, her eyes scanning the room. "Any discussion must take place with fewer listening ears."

Sörnam's black eyes widened then narrowed. "I want everyone to leave this room. NOW!"

The room emptied without protest. Angerwin wasted no time stating her terms.

"I want to be freed from your curse in exchange for the Stone of Power."

"How do you know of the curse?" Sörnam asked, sitting forward in his throne.

"I am no fool, Sörnam, and neither are the other people here. Your people know of the evil you have brought upon them. They stay, not from loyalty, but because of the curse that binds them to you."

Sörnam laughed disdainfully.

"The curse has always been my best idea. Each of the leaders before me had their own holds upon this army, but of course, mine is the most powerful. When Palmer ruled, the army was weak and wavering. The people were cowards, unwilling to finish the war they themselves had started. But they feared me, so much so, that when I came to power, I used their fear to control every last one of them.

Their fear fuels the curse, strengthens it, but alas, it seems to be less effective on stubborn dragons."

Angerwin let out a low growl.

"I no longer fear you as I once did."

"We shall see," he replied with a cold laugh.

Angerwin roared, and the throne room shook.

"Long have I tried to break completely free, but your curse holds me still. I want nothing more than to be free from you!"

Sörnam's face twisted with evil glee.

"You will leave me now to consider your proposition. I will give you your answer in the morning."

Angerwin left Sörnam, relieved. Alone, she thought back to the moment, weeks earlier, when she had attempted to escape Sörnam's grasp—a moment when her fortunes changed.

She fled Phärnam, flying frantically and with no clear direction. Over the mountains and into unknown terrain she flew, weary and scared, yet unwilling to turn back. The weather turned treacherous, and she knew she must seek shelter. Spotting a cave in the mountainside, she hid from the violent wind and rain.

"Who dares enter my cave?" a menacing voice growled.

At the sight of the cave's occupant, Angerwin bowed deeply and spoke with great respect, "I am Angerwin, Dragon of Fire. I am honored, Drinin, Guardian of Sea and Trees, to be in your presence. I ask forgiveness, for I did not know this to be your cave. The raging storm forced me to find shelter, or I would not have intruded."

Drinin stopped her. "Fear not. You are welcome here. Rest as long as you need."

Angerwin inclined her head in thanks and settled onto the cave's cold floor.

"May I ask a question?" asked Drinin.

Angerwin nodded.

"Why is it that you are so far away from Sŏrnam? I hear tell of the great loyalty Sŏrnam's subjects have for him. Why then, does your aura tell a different story?"

Angerwin gave a gloomy laugh.

"Sŏrnam has bound us to him with a great curse. We must live, knowing ourselves powerless against him and unable to fight his will. His hold strengthens as our fear grows, and so we live to fear our master, and hate festers in our hearts. None can break free, and few have strength enough to speak of it."

Drinin smiled kindly. "And yet, here you are."

"His curse falls weak upon my being, as I grow to fear him less and less. Still, I cannot break entirely free and must do his bidding should he command it. For now, his mind is full of other matters, and he spares little thought on me. My time becomes more and more my own, and thus I hold the power to escape, but only temporarily."

There was a brief silence before Drinin spoke, "What if there was a way to break away from the curse?"

Angerwin laughed mirthlessly.

"I would do almost anything to be free."

"What if you were to make a deal with him? What if, in exchange for your freedom, you offer him the location of the Stone of Power? I know of a map in Bahra's possession that gives the Stone's location. If I could get you the map, you could trade it for your freedom."

Angerwin stared at Drinin, aghast. "Y-you would have me betray this land for my own freedom? Are you not bound to this land? To serve and protect its interests?"

Drinin smiled wisely. "You mistake me, dear one. Your freedom is valuable, but the cost is not what you imagine. Sŏrnam will find the stone, with or without the map. We give him what he seeks, not to further his cause, but to control how he seeks it. The Children of the Prophecy are among us. The time has come, and we must play our part."

The plan was set into motion with surprising ease. Word was sent to Bahra and Arron, fears were alleviated, and details were secured. Angerwin found herself returning to Phärnam, a key player in a daring plot that could destroy them all or save Thurnangl from the cusp of destruction.

Angerwin sat atop Sŭrnam's castle, deep in thought.

The young dragon, Hallin, perched next to her. "Why do you not practice with us, Angerwin? Have you been trying to fly away again?" Hallin laughed at his joke.

"There is no need for stupidity, Hallin," hissed Calina.

Hallin shrank from the wrath of the elder dragon, Calina. He was small, and young with very little skill in battle. He was unremarkable in every aspect, his scales the color of dry dull mud and his intellect barely sufficient. Calina, hovering next to him, was a fearsome sight to behold with the moonlight reflecting off of her indigo scales. She surpassed even Drinin in age and experience, and she used her years of misery as a weapon against her foes.

"I've been," Angerwin paused, "Preoccupied."

"It matters not to us," Calina sneered. "We have no need of you."

The terrible dragon flew away dismissively.

"Gracious," Hallin sighed, "Why must she always be angry? So, what HAVE you been doing, Angerwin?"

Angerwin studied Hallin carefully. He was so young and ignorant of the ways of this world. She couldn't tell him of their plans, and yet she wished she could save him from what was to come.

"I have been training alone," she said.

"Well, if you want a sparring partner, let me know," Hallin said as he flew off.

I promise I will try to free you as well, my little brother.

Angerwin remained on her perch throughout the night. As the sun stretched over the tree tops, she breathed in the beauty, steeling herself for the ordeal ahead. The magnificent sight of all that lay before her in the golden morning light gave her courage. Today would be the dawn of hope for her and many others.

Making her way to the throne room, Angerwin approached Sörnam where he sat, alone, on the throne.

"What is your decision, Sörnam?"

Sörnam stood from his throne and walked to Angerwin, extending his hand.

"I have decided to accept your offer."

For a moment, Angerwin hesitated, but she knew she must not falter. She passed the true map to Sörnam who responded with a single word, "Deconte."

Angerwin was free. The darkness that had clouded her eyes for so long dispersed revealing orbs of the fieriest red. She breathed a sigh of relief.

Sörnam turned, an evil grin upon his face. "It is quite foolish, you know, to join my enemies even as you stand before me."

He snapped his fingers and magically unveiled fifty guards, swords drawn, surrounding Angerwin. The dragon roared, blue flame spewing from her jaws, incinerating the guards and opening the ceiling to her escape. She turned to Sörnam, huddled in defense against her flame, and laughed before flying away.

Sörnam studied the map in his hand, and cackled madly. "My conquest is almost complete."

Crystal and Brant stood up, as did everyone else. There was another knock on the door. Crystal went to answer the door, Brant following close behind.

Crystal opened the door, and there in the doorway stood Arron beaming as bright as the light from the sun shining down upon him.

"Arron!" Crystal exclaimed.

"It's nice to see you again," said Brant as he walked up behind her.

Arron clasped Crystal's hand, smiling.

"I come bearing great news. May I come in, please?"

Crystal and Brant led him to the kitchen.

When Frinz saw Arron, her heart leapt with joy. She sprang up from her seat and jumped into his outstretched arms.

"Arron it is wondrous to see you again."

Realizing they had an audience, Frinz composed herself.

"What news have you brought us?" Frinz asked eagerly.

"We have a plan," he said with a sparkle in his eyes.

The group listened eagerly as Arron recounted Angerwin's meeting with Drinin.

"Angerwin has provided the enemy with the location of the Stone of Power. A trap has been set."

"WHAT?!" Frinz and Liane said in unison.

"But why? Why not just give him a false location or something so that we won't endanger the Stone of Power?" Liane asked.

"This war began with the Stone of Power, and so it shall end. We believe Sörnam's greed will blind him to our trap and provide us the opening we need to strike. His entire army marches to the Stone, and we shall meet them at Silver Town. We are gathering our forces to intercept the army. Sürnam thinks that we cannot stop him, but we will."

They stood silently for a moment as they considered the plan.

"I wish someone would have told us sooner," Brant said, feeling a twinge of anxiety.

"It's not like we have a choice, and I for one agree. I want this to end now. Besides, this army is not led by just us three," Crystal said.

Frinz sighed, "I must also agree. Now is the time to end this, once and for all. We have an opening so let us strike. Arron, how soon will Sürnam's army arrive at Silver Town?"

"In two days," Arron replied. "We should leave as soon as you are ready to—,"

"We're ready," Crystal and Brant said together.

This was their final test, the reason for all that had come before. They would fight with all they had. Something deep inside Crystal and Brant burned. They gathered everything they would need. Crystal was almost shaking with nervousness.

Brant held her hands and said, "Everything is going to be ok. We will fight and win, together"

Crystal took a deep breath and nodded.

Liane, Mardra, and Whiticker would stay behind.

They stood outside saying their goodbyes, giving words of hope and embraces of luck.

"You will be ok, right?" Whiticker asked.

Crystal hugged him. "I sure hope so."

Mardra kissed Crystal and Brant them on the forehead.

"We will pray for your safe return. Fulfill your destiny. Save our people."

The travelers set off, Brant and Crystal waving from Zabrina's back until they could see their friends no more. Frinz rode with Arron, relishing their time together. The journey to Silver Town would take many hours—many hours in which each would fathom their victory, or their demise.

CHAPTER 28

A BATTLE OF GREAT PROPORTIONS

The plains stretched out below them—a sea of green, grassy waves rolling gently with the wind. They flew over the very same field they had walked through upon their arrival in Thurnangl. It seemed so long ago that Crystal and Brant had followed Frinz as they began the journey to fulfill the Prophecy. So much had changed, and now, it would all end at this very spot.

They spotted Silver Town below, surrounded by thousands of white tents. Smoke rose from the various fires around camp as witches and wizards hurried about, preparing for battle. Brant and Crystal slid from Zabrina's back as she landed, eager to join the army in its preparations.

Crystal looked to Zabrina. "Is there a way you could get Drinin and Angerwin to meet us here later? We must discuss our plans, but first, Brant and I are going to find Lilly."

Zabrina nodded and flew to find her fellow dragons.

Crystal looked at Brant with a worried smile, "Let's go."

They walked about, stopping to speak with many witches and wizards, but no one had seen the young woman with the rare pink eyes. Crystal scanned the crowd, sure that Lilly must be near. They had promised to find each other. A musical voice rose above the crowd, and Crystal turned to see her friend rushing toward her.

"Crystal!" called Lilly. She ran swiftly, colliding with Crystal and squeezed her in a tight embrace. "I am so pleased to see you once more!

Crystal returned Lilly's warm hug.

"Lilly, I would like to introduce you to Brant."

Brant bowed to Lilly gratefully, "Thank you for saving our lives."

Lilly ruffled Brant's hair.

"We have saved more than just three lives here Brant."

"Lilly!" shouted a voice nearby.

Crystal and Brant looked up to see a tall man, fully clad in armor, making his way through the crowd. His orange eyes were focused directly on Lilly, as if she were the only woman in the world.

"Lilly! There you are," he said, pulling her close.

"Crystal and Brant, I would like you to meet Basem," Lilly said.

Crystal and Brant bowed deeply to Basem who laughed.

"I should indeed bow to you, Children of the Prophecy. You helped free the one person most precious to me. For that, I humbly thank you."

"Lilly," Crystal motioned to her friend, "we must speak privately. There is much to discuss before battle."

Zabrina landed on the outskirts of the camp and sought out Drinin. She found him in deep conversation with Frinz and Arron. He was, to Zabrina's surprise, accompanied by Angerwin. The group made quite a spectacle, and nearby onlookers could not help but gawk at the three mighty dragons and their human companions.

"Angerwin and Drinin...I had not thought to find you together... to see you speaking so intimately," Zabrina said, barely concealing her smile.

"Yes," Angerwin said, bowing, "I must apologize for my past actions. No apology will undo the harm I have caused, but I do intend to help end this war."

Zabrina smiled, "You have helped so much already, and we thank you."

Angerwin blushed, and Drinin nudged her as if to say, "I told you so."

"Crystal and Brant would like to speak with you both. Frinz and Arron are meant to come as well."

Zabrina led the group through camp to the place where Crystal waited with Brant and their new friends. Introductions were made, and Arron led them away from camp to a secluded location where they could speak freely. They spent the day planning, arguing logistics, and learning as much as they could about their enemy. Lilly did her best to answer their questions about her brother and the forces he commanded. The task gave her pain, but she was determined to help.

"One thing I don't quite understand," Crystal said to Lilly during a lull in their conversation, "Sörnam's curse. Why didn't it affect you?"

Lilly laughed softly and spoke to the group at large, "I was never afraid of Sörnam. When I was young, he was simply my older brother, and I had no understanding of what he truly was. Even as I grew and began to understand, I hated him more than I feared him. The curse overtook Crystal when she lost her hope, and in so doing, it used her link with Brant to cripple him. When Crystal regained her hope, she was able to fight through the curse, but her link with Brant had been severed, and so she could not reach through and bring him out of his despair. He was locked away by Sörnam's curse."

There was a heavy silence, and Crystal gazed sadly at Brant.

Brant kissed her gently.

"There is no use worrying about it anymore. What happened in the past is over and done, and you and I are alright. That is what matters."

It took many hours to finalize their plan, but they knew it to be a great one.

The group retired for the evening to seek sleeping quarters, but sleep did not come swiftly for Crystal and Brant. They lay awake, listening to the faint call ringing through their ears and hearts. What called them, they knew not, but they knew that soon they must follow. The call stopped as suddenly as it had begun, and the pair drifted into dreamless sleep.

Crystal and Brant woke early the next morning and left Frinz to rest. They walked the streets of the quiet town, holding hands and hoping that this was not their last day together.

They heard the blow of a horn across town and ran toward the sound. At the edge of town stood an army, one hundred strong. The Entremdor had come carrying spears, bows, and swords. Leading their march was Bahra.

"Crystal, Brant," she bowed, "it is a pleasure to see you once more."

Arron joined them, addressing Bahra gratefully, "I am pleased that you have come."

"We offer you our service. We fight for the freedom of our people and this land," Bahra said, and her people gave a loud roar of excitement.

As more and more people and tribes joined the army preparing for battle, spirits in the camp climbed. Voices were raised in laughter and song as all worked to prepare. The day began to draw to a close, and a nervous energy thrummed through the camp. The coming dawn would bring battle unlike any they'd seen before, and many lay awake late into the night.

Once more, the unknown call beckoned to Crystal and Brant until they were unable to rest.

Crystal, sighed, "I know it's early, but let's go…it's better to be there early than late, right?"

Brant chuckled and said, "Fine, maybe we'll find what has been calling to us."

They gathered their supplies and armed themselves, bowing for a moment in prayer before slipping quietly from the inn. Looking over the sleeping town, they smiled. The outcome of the battle was unknown, but Crystal and Brant knew they would not give up on these people, no matter what.

The night air was crisp and clear, scented with the sweet breeze and lit dimly by sparkling stars above. Crystal flew them on the wind, nearer and nearer to the final place of battle and the stone that would draw Sörnam. Dawn was peeking over the horizon when they reached the small hill marked as the place where good would meet evil.

The unknown call returned, pulsing loudly between them as they descended to earth, but it stopped the moment their feet touched down. For a moment, all was still. Then quietly, ever so quietly, the sound began again. Crystal and Brant looked to the earth below their feet and then to one another.

"The Stone of Power," they said together.

"But why would it call us here?" Crystal asked.

Brant thought for a moment.

"Maybe——," he began, as the idea came to him, "wait, do you remember what Frinz told us? That the Stone of Power is a life source to, not only the people, but the land as well? Maybe the land is scared too. It knows Sörnam is coming, and it knows we are here to fight him."

Crystal considered quietly, "I guess everything is scared of Sörnam huh?"

"Well just about. Personally, I'm looking forward to ending him."

Crystal laughed and shivered.

Frinz shook her head at the empty beds before her. She was neither surprised nor alarmed, but still she worried for them. Squaring her shoulders, she rose to face the day. Many would count on her strength this day, and she would not disappointment them. Frinz stepped from the inn into the flurry of preparation.

Arron was waiting for her in full armor. "Ready?" he asked, offering his hand.

She smiled confidently, taking his warm hand. "Yes, I am."

Arron ordered his troops into position and raised the banners high. Bahra stood tall and proud with her Entremdor behind her, ready to lead the charge into battle.

The black line of Sörnam's army grew closer and closer as the sun rose in the early morning sky. On the ground marched the dark forces, cursed to do his bidding, while Sörnam himself flew regally above, riding Calina. Behind him sat Aaliyah, cool and aloof.

Angerwin frowned at the sight of the young dragon, Hallin, flying swiftly by Calina's side. She wished more for him than the horrors of war, and she prayed she would not see him breathe his last breath this day.

Arron did not hesitate. He gave his troops the signal to attack. The time for waiting was over. As the armies collided with the clashes and cries of battle, the earth shook with the finality of this fight.

Frinz deflected a spell flying toward her and looked up to see Calina flying overhead.

"Zabrina!" Frinz shouted, blocking another spell.

Zabrina flew into the air and stopped before Calina.

"You will not pass," Zabrina growled, baring her teeth.

Aaliyah and Sürnam only laughed.

"I will take her, master," Calina said, her eyes never leaving Zabrina.

Sürnam and Aaliyah jumped from Calina's back and disappeared into thin air.

Zabrina blinked as they disappeared, and Calina attacked, sinking her teeth into Zabrina's neck. Zabrina bellowed and lashed out at her foe, sending them both toward the ground below. They fought and clawed, tearing flesh and drawing blood, until Calina caught Zabrina and hurled her to the ground. Zabrina fell but recovered and came at Calina fiercely, flame on her lips.

Arron fought side by side with his beloved, slashing and slicing even as Frinz deflected the magic that soared around them. At every turn, new enemies approached, but Arron's aim was true with every stroke of his sword. "My dear," he shouted, "it is as we expected! Sürnam goes to the Stone and he will be well met!"

"Our plan was sound," Frinz replied, blasting a line of oncoming soldiers with explosive magic.

"I did not think they would teleport so soon, but," she grunted as she deflected another spell and used it to strike an oncoming soldier, "they will be met with a fight!"

Flames rained down from the dragons fighting above, scorching the blood-soaked ground. Many wizards and witches caught fire, and screams could be heard from all around as they burned.

Frinz shielded herself and Arron from the fire

"Let us hope that we survive this battle," she said.

Angerwin was fighting Hallin, as Drinin was going to the rear of Sürnam's army destroying as many wizards and witches as he could. The fields were lit with fire, and the air was filled with thick smoke. As visibility decreased, many were forced to use less magic and fight with the weapons they carried. Hallin and Angerwin circled each other, neither prepared to strike first. Hallin broke the silence.

"Why?" he shouted. "You left, and you did not even say goodbye! We are family! I would have understood!"

Angerwin growled, "I could say nothing. You and I both know that! The curse was still upon me as it is still upon you now."

Hallin stared at Angerwin with the cold, dead eyes of the accursed.

"I have been ordered to kill you, and so I must."

Hallin flew forward, spewing thick flames before him. Angerwin countered with her own powerful blue flame, and their fire collided, sending thick clouds of smoke through the air. Angerwin peered through the haze but could see nothing.

Hallin surprised her, sinking his teeth into her neck from behind. Angerwin roared in pain, her blue flame striking the ground below and destroying all it touched. The dragons tumbled through the air and hit the ground roughly, Hallin's jaw still clasped on Angerwin's neck. She scratched and clawed, but he could not be moved. Opening her jaws, Angerwin attacked with the only weapon powerful enough to loosen his grip—her flame. It hit Hallin in the face, and he let go of her neck, collapsing on the ground. He did not move as Angerwin approached, battered and bleeding.

"I did not wish to kill you," she wheezed.

She stood for a moment breathing heavily, and Hallin jumped to attack once more.

"You did not!" he roared, opening his mouth.

Fire raged at Angerwin, striking her in the face. The dragons flew into the air, roaring as they collided again and ripping at each other's scales. Blood rained down onto the ground below.

Crystal and Brant could feel the battle raging far from where they stood. They made ready for their own fight and awaited Sörnam's arrival. They would not wait long. Sörnam appeared before them with Aaliyah at his side, and all braced for what was to come.

"Well, well, it looks as though we have been expected after all. This will be a treat, will it not? To kill the Children of the Prophecy, the two who were to end it all." Sörnam laughed icily.

"I'll take Sörnam," Crystal whispered.

"No way in hell! He's mine!" Brant screamed as he rushed forward. The field around them was set ablaze, and the flames sent smoke pouring through the air.

Brant sent a dozen jagged rocks flying toward Sörnam, but the evil wizard extended his hand surrounding himself with a magical shield. Striking the shield, the rocks turned to dust. Brant tried moving the ground under his enemy's feet, but as the ground shot up, Sörnam mealy moved nimbly to stand atop it. Sörnam smiled wickedly and pointed a finger at Brant. He uttered an incantation, and from his finger shot a bolt of lightning. Brant parried with jets of hot lava.

Crystal soared through the air toward Aaliyah, bringing down her sword. Aaliyah dodged the blade and cast an illusion spell.

Crystal looked around at Aaliyah's mirages surrounding her and laughed, "That's not going to work this time!"

Ice shards rained down upon every illusion as Crystal sought Aaliyah's true form. Mirages flickered away as the ice slashed through them, until Aaliyah stood before Crystal, her body cut and bleeding. Crystal sent a giant block of ice flying forward, and Aaliyah jumped away, reciting another incantation.

The world around Crystal turned black, and she could see nothing. There was no way to know when or how Aaliyah would strike next, for Crystal was consumed by utter darkness. Brant saw Crystal scrambling blindly and knew he must help.

"Crystal! In front of you!" he shouted as he set Sörnam's cape ablaze.

Crystal lunged forward, and her sword pierced flesh. Aaliyah sneered as she studied her wound, but the hit had served its purpose. The spell was broken, and Crystal's eyesight was restored. Aaliyah stepped forward, a new spell on her lips, but Crystal lunged once more.

It was as though the world ceased to spin. For one moment, Aaliyah looked down and then back to Crystal in surprise. The sword had run clean through, and Aaliyah fell to her knees, clinging to what little life was left. She turned to find her master, but Sörnam spared her only the smallest of glances. Aaliyah's eye softened, and as death came, she felt relieved to finally be free of her beloved master once and for all. Tears rolled down her face.

"Peace," she whispered, falling to the ground.

All was still, and Aaliyah lay dead. Crystal rushed to Brant's side. Now, it was two against one. Sörnam's face was a mass of amusement as he surveyed the children before him.

"Oh, I see," he hissed, "you think to overpower me, but you are mistaken. For now, the fun truly begins."

CHAPTER 29

DARKNESS ENDS

The battle at Silver Town raged on the ground and in the sky. Zabrina collided with Calina once more, and the dragons battled fiercely. Calina brought unmatched strength to the fight, but Zabrina's cunning and healing abilities made them equally matched.

They bobbed and weaved through the air, each determined to fell the other. Calina's claw found Zabrina's eye, and she ripped it from the socket, evoking a howl of agony. Zabrina fought back, slashing at Calina's chest until blood poured from the wound. She lunged forward once more, a claw tearing fiercely through one of Calina's wings. The mighty dragon faltered, but remained aloft, wincing with every beat of her wings.

Zabrina knew she could not continue much longer, for her strength was waning, and she had already lost much of her healing ability. The eye she had lost could not regenerate fully, and Zabrina knew she must finish her opponent or she would surely perish. Calina laughed as she studied Zabrina's pathetic form, bruised and battered before her. Zabrina opened her jaws and released a fiery flame that Calina easily dodged, but it was enough. Calina's momentary distraction allowed Zabrina to lunge unnoticed, and she clamped onto the elder dragon's purple neck with the last of her strength.

They plummeted to the ground, Zabrina's jaws clamped firmly on her enemy's throat. The impact was abrupt and painful, but still she held firm until the last breath left Calina's body.

Zabrina stared down at Calina's motionless form, her breath heaving and unsteady. She had little energy and no words left to speak. Content in her victory, she let herself collapse. Through the haze of the battlefield, Frinz saw her fall.

"Arron!" she shouted frantically, "Over there! Zabrina!"

Frinz ran toward her friend, blasting all who stood in her way. Arron followed, slicing at any who would harm Frinz as she ran toward the injured dragon. Zabrina lay barely conscious, her body bruised and broken. Frinz could see that all of the dragon's effort could not heal the wounds fast enough.

"Is there anything we can do?" Frinz whispered.

Zabrina gasped with pain and shook her head. "No, dear Frinz, you must not worry. I shall find cover and gather my strength. Go now, and fight."

Frinz nodded tearfully and kissed Zabrina. "Be well, my brave Zabrina."

Frinz used the smallest bit of magic to help her friend escape the battlefield. Zabrina found her strength restored just enough to fly to the outlying fields. There, she hid to rest and recover.

The smoke swirled thick around Frinz and Arron. Nodding to one another, they ran from its cover and into the fight.

Arron's sword sliced through people as if they were made of water. Frinz saw a small group of attackers, out of the corner of her eye, approaching at great speed. She stopped her progress to cast a spell, but a woman stepped into the path before her. The woman enchanted the grass beneath the enemy's feet and it crept toward them, wrapping around their throats and strangling them.

"Thank you," Frinz said as she turned to fight on.

The woman nodded before running off into the fray.

The sun was now high overhead, its rays beating down on the armor-clad soldiers. The smoke on the battlefield was thick and stifling. Her throat scorched, Frinz coughed and choked from the thick haze, unaware that the enemy was upon her. A sword ripped through her armor, leaving a gash across her back. She screamed in pain as she fell to her knees. The blood from her wound soaked the shirt beneath her armor, and tears welled as her assailant stood over her.

"Well, well, Princess Frinz, it looks as if your journey ends here," the man laughed, slicing once more through her armor.

Frinz screamed and awaited the blow she knew would come next. She felt the swish of the sword, but it did not meet her flesh again. Before her stood Arron, his eyes brimming with fire as he stared down the man who had assaulted his love.

With a swish of his sword, Arron severed the man's head, watching it roll into the surround flames. The useless body fell to the ground, limp and lifeless. Arron touched Frinz's injured back, and she winced.

"I am so sorry," he whispered.

She reached up painfully and touched his face with a trembling hand.

"It is not—," She coughed as blood trickled down from the side of her mouth, "not your fault, Arron."

Frinz smiled weakly and continued, "I cannot even feel it anymore, but Arron…"

Arron brought her hand to his face. Tears poured from his eyes.

"Please you must not leave me. Not you too, my love," he pleaded.

Frinz gave a weak sigh.

"I am so sorry," her voice grew quieter with each word, "but please Arron, know… I… I love you."

With that, Frinz closed her eyes.

Arron knew he must act, and fast. He could not let her die, not now. He removed the armor from her torso and scooped Frinz's lifeless body into his arms. Blood continued to run from her wounds, soaking her shirt and his arms. He ran swiftly, seeking a healer but knowing not where one might be. His thoughts turned to Zabrina, and he drew the tiny chain from beneath Frinz's shirt. He prayed the dragon was well enough to heed his call.

He was about to blow the whistle when he was met with a hoard of black-armored wizards, thirsty for blood.

Holding Frinz in one arm, he brandished his sword with the other and cried, "Let me PASS!"

He brought down his sword with a mighty swing and a surge of magic burst forth, sending his enemies flying from him. Arron could not stop to think what had brought him such power. He drew the whistle to his lips and blew forcefully, knowing the dragon must hear for Frinz to live.

Zabrina was still regaining her strength when the call came, and she wasted no time in answering. Flying to the source, she saw Arron with Frinz's lifeless body in his arms, and she feared the worst. Landing as close as possible, she dispatched the surrounding enemy and turned to her dear friend.

The love that radiated from Zabrina worked its magic, and the healing process began almost instantly. The wound on Frinz's back sewed itself together, and the shattered bones of her shoulder mended quickly. A jagged scar was all that remained of the wound, but still Frinz did not wake.

"She has lost far too much blood. We must take her to a safe place to rest," Zabrina said.

Arron nodded and climbed onto Zabrina's back, holding Frinz tightly. Zabrina flew off into the fields, and Arron remained with them as his love continued to heal. They waited, watching intently for Frinz to wake.

Angerwin fell to the ground, hitting it with such great force that one of her back legs snapped. Blood continued to pour from her wounds, and the dragon's breathing grew labored. She studied Hallin, who was in similarly bad condition. Large patches of scales and skin were missing from his body, and the tip of his tale was completely removed. He winced with each breath as though his ribs were broken.

"Hallin," Angerwin pleaded, "please. I do not wish to kill you!"

Hallin's eyes turned to slits, "You know…I have no choice," he said coldly. "I am bound by this curse."

"But you do, Hallin! I know how strong you are, and I know that you can fight this," Angerwin pleaded.

Hallin struggled to speak, as though he choked on the words that came from his lips. "I have tried…I still try…to turn from the curse. My soul screams, but my body is bound here. His will is too strong. We are not all like you, able to turn away."

Sörnam has given Hallin a direct order to kill me. This may not work, but I have to try. Angerwin thought.

"Hallin," Angerwin said, struggling to breathe, "You have to try and fight this."

"NO!" Hallin screamed, shooting another flame at Angerwin who had no strength to dodge it. She closed her eyes, but the flame did not reach her. Drinin stood before her, the searing flames blasting him brutally.

"Drinin?!"

"Worry not," the ancient dragon roared over the flames, "I am old enough to withstand the fire of such a young dragon."

Angerwin looked to Hallin who winced at Drinin's words.

"You should not protect the likes of her, Drinin. She is a traitor to her kind! She did not even try to save us! She was only concerned with freeing herself from the bonds of the curse."

Drinin gave a low laugh.

"She is no traitor. She chose her freedom and fought for it. I see you are too weak to do the same."

"You know that I can do no such thing," Hallin said quietly.

"But why?" Angerwin asked. "I was able to break free. Why then should you not do the same?"

Drinin watched as Hallin looked from his opponents to the ground.

Hallin winced and fell back. He knew himself beholden and bound to Sörnam and could see no escape. From Hallin's infancy, the evil lord had always been there, guiding and teaching, punishing and instilling fear.

"No. I cannot go against Sörnam's order. I cannot disobey commands," Hallin said in a shaky voice.

"Then you have chosen your fate," Drinin roared, rearing back and opening his massive jaws.

Angerwin ran to stand in front of the young dragon.

"Please," she pleaded, "he is so young. You must not kill him because of the fear that binds him. Please, Drinin, there has to be another way!"

Drinin smiled and said, "Precisely."

He flew with incredible speed past Angerwin's stricken form and spewed fire into Hallin's shocked face. The young dragon toppled and did not move.

"NO!" Angerwin screamed as she ran to Hallin's side. His body was limp and motionless.

"Drinin, how…how could you?!" Angerwin bared her teeth and tensed to spring at Drinin.

He merely chuckled. "There was nothing more to be done. He shall sleep soundly until the battle is finished."

"He is not dead?" Angerwin asked, studying Hallin's lifeless form.

Drinin laughed once more, "No. I would never kill someone who is precious to you, Angerwin."

Angerwin was relieved to have her young brother safe at last. Drinin notice her still-bleeding wounds and the way she winced as she moved.

"You must tend to your wounds now," he said. "Find Zabrina, and do not fear for Hallin. I will take him where no harm may come to him.

Angerwin nodded her thanks and flew to find Zabrina. She surveyed the battlefield below, saddened by the sea of dead bodies before her. Smoke billowed around her, bringing the scent of death and burning. Though she flew the course of the battlefield, Angerwin did not see Zabrina, and her concern mounted.

She forged ahead but soon grew weary. Her wounds were draining what strength she had left. Knowing she must rest, Angerwin moved toward the fields surrounding the battleground. There, she spotted Zabrina and the lifeless form of Frinz, clasped tight in Arron's arms. Fear struck her heart, and she made to land near her friends. She could feel her wounds healing almost instantly.

"What has happened?" Angerwin asked fearfully.

Frinz stirred.

"Frinz? Are you alright, my love?" Arron asked gently.

Frinz's eyes fluttered open, and she gazed at the concerned faces surrounding her.

"I am much improved," she whispered, "though I still feel the blade that pierced my skin, even as the pain dwindles."

"You will feel the wounds as they heal, as though they remain open. Yet you will feel no pain. Perhaps you should rest," Zabrina suggested.

"No, I must not," Frinz asserted. "I shall not rest until the battle is won!"

Arron sighed and smiled at Frinz.

"I cannot stop you, so I will fight by your side."

Zabrina opened her wings and turned to them with a deep growl.

"Let us end this battle!"

The Children of the Prophecy stood before Sörnam. Crystal hurled ice shards in Sörnam's direction, but he deflected them with a protective shield. The ice turned to water and fell to the ground. Brant laid his hand on Crystal's shoulder as she moved to strike once more. Brant inhaled, focusing intently as he pulled molten lava from deep beneath their feet. With a simple flick of his wrist, the magma engulfed Sörnam.

Crystal acted quickly, pulling as much water as she could from the vegetation at their feet, and doused the mount of molten liquid. The lava turned black and hardened. All was still.

Crystal and Brant sighed with relief, but as Crystal turned into Brant's embrace, a cracking sound was heard. The lava shell erupted violently, sending shards of basalt soaring around them. Brant pulled Crystal to the ground, covering them with a hovering boulder and shielding them from falling shrapnel.

Sörnam stood, breathing heavily but unharmed by the heavy blow.

Crystal rose again to attack, twisting and sending hundreds of ice shards flying at him. She prayed that the winds were in her favor. Sörnam's laugh turned to a gasp as her ice dagger breeched his shield and sliced through his shoulder. All was silent for a moment as they stared at each other. Was Sörnam growing weaker, or were the Children of the Prophecy growing stronger together?

Sürnam studied his bleeding arm and stepped forward, the sinister smile returning to his face. With a flick of his hand, Sürnam launched Crystal through the air. Her ice was no match for his lightning force. She rose, her head spinning, as Sürnam laughed and turned. Brant was running toward her, his back turned from their enemy. Crystal lifted her hand in warning, but time had run out.

"Amzelo."

Crystal saw Brant's eyes widen and his body go limp as he fell to the ground. She was next to him in a second and turned him over. Brant lay lifeless and unmoving, his eyes closed and unblinking. Crystal put her shaking hand on his heart, but there was no beat. Her eyes swam with tears as she sought to heal his broken body, but it was no use.

No, no this can't....happen...this wasn't supposed to happen... this has to be wrong....

Crystal sat stunned, her world crumbling around her. Outside the walls of her personal pain, she could vaguely hear Sürnam's harsh laugh.

"My, but this is fun! I never dreamed it would be so easy."

Crystal could think of nothing to say. She wanted nothing but Brant. The tears were streaming from her eyes as she clung to his lifeless body.

"Lilly!" Crystal shouted as loud as she could.

Sürnam's eyes widened, and then he cackled. "Do you think such a weakling can save you? HA!"

"I am no weakling," said a voice behind Sürnam.

He turned to see Lilly standing before him.

"Lilly? How in the world did you—,"

"Save your questions, brother. Today I have come to end you." Lilly spoke quietly, her words cutting through the air like knives.

Sörnam only laughed louder.

Lilly's sudden smile silenced him.

"You laugh, but it is true. You have never known my power, for you were too obsessed with your own. Watch now, brother, and I will show you what I have learned."

Sörnam threw his head back in a fit of hysterical laughter.

"You? The mere child I raised? I taught you everything you know. You live because of my mercy."

He paused, his smile falling from his lips, "Perhaps that was a mistake."

"Hentach, Amzelo, Erento!" Lilly shouted, standing firm.

An immense wave of power shimmered around her.

Sörnam stood as if transfixed as fire flooded his veins and every last breath left his lungs. Lilly stepped closer and smiled down at the evil man, beaten by his own magic.

"You have no power, no authority, nothing. No trace of you will be left in this land but the dust of your body carried in the wind. Goodbye, brother."

The world turned black for the vile rule. A triumphant, breathtaking Lilly was the last sight he beheld. His body, consumed by the very evil he had created, turned to black dust and blew away in the soft summer breeze.

Lilly sighed and closed her eyes, relishing the freedom of their victory. No longer did the burden of her brother's evil weigh heavy on her heart. She was free.

The sun was low in the sky, casting shadows on the war-torn land, as a great shudder came over the battlefield. Arron's army stared in wonder as their enemy stood before them, frozen in place.

A sudden light came upon Sörnam's soldiers, and as one, they blinked away the curse that had consumed them. Gone were the dead eyes of the accursed, replaced by vibrant life once more. The men turned to one another, each his own person once more, tears streaming from bright eyes. Enemies embraced, and the curse's hold on the people of Thurnangl was vanquished completely. They were free at last.

Shouts of triumph filled the air, and enemies were now brothers. Frinz jumped into Arron's arms and kissed him fiercely. The Great War was over, and Thurnangl was whole once more.

Basem looked up at the sky and smiled. "She did it."

The cheers did not reach the weeping Crystal who sat, clinging to her love's lifeless body. Brant had not moved nor breathed, and Crystal was inconsolable. Lilly touched the young girl's shoulder, knowing no words could afford comfort.

"We made a promise..." Crystal whispered around her sobs. "We made a promise that we would stay together forever."

Lilly could feel her own tears coming as she stood silently watching her friend weep in anguish. They remained that way for a long while, and when Lilly next looked up, the sun was setting low in the sky.

"Crystal?" Lilly asked.

"I...won't leave Brant's side...I won't..." Crystal whimpered.

Lilly could say no more.

"Brant," Crystal cried, "we made a promise....so please... Come back... I can't do this without you by my side."

In Crystal's anguish, her voice rang out in musical lament. Her melody surrounded them, a slow agonizing song flowing from the depths of her soul. Her pain mingled with her voice in an eloquent dance, a sound both beautiful and heartbreaking. She clutched his shirt with trembling hands, her head resting on his lifeless chest, as the final notes of her song danced around them.

For a moment, Crystal thought she felt a flutter in his chest. She opened her eyes and sat up, her gaze never leaving his face. A gasp escaped her lips as Brant's limp body took in breath. The color flooded back to his face, and his eyes fluttered open. Brant propped himself up carefully, chuckling.

"Aw man, I missed the good part, didn't I?"

Tears ran freely down Crystal's face, as she gasped, "How in the—,"

Brant beamed. "It was easy. I had a beautiful voice to guide me back." He wiped away her tears and whispered, "I love you."

Crystal was still crying, but this time from joy.

"I love you too"

Their kiss was interrupted by Lilly's tearful embrace.

"Brant!? I thought for sure you were lost to us!" she said, sobbing with joy.

They hugged each other tightly and couldn't help but laugh. It was all over.

"Crystal," prompted Brant, "let's say we give one last gift to Thurnangl, as a thank you to the people."

"I was thinking the same thing!" she replied.

Crystal and Brant walked to the top of the hill where the Stone of Power lay, buried deep within. Brant held out his hands, and a small blue light shone from the ground. Brant and Crystal clasped hands, concentrating. The blue light sprang from the ground, and the force that had called them forth was revealed. A tiny blue crystal rose from its hiding place and floated before them, pulsing with magic and power.

The Children of the Prophecy closed their eyes and gave back the energy the Stone of Power had bestowed upon them. Receiving their gift, the Stone of Power grew until it was four feet long. In a flash of light, it radiated throughout the land, touching every living thing.

When it had finished, the light faded, and the stone sank, completed at last, back from whence it came.

Brant and Crystal fell, laughing, to the ground. Lilly found them a short time later, fast asleep. She smiled as she blessed them, for no sleep was ever more deserved.

CHAPTER 30
A GOODBYE NOT FOREVER

Brant woke to the warmth and glow of the sun shining upon him, a feeling he thought never to experience again. He stretched, relishing in it, and watched Crystal sleeping in her bed.

I never thought I would see her shining face again, he thought

Crystal woke to find him studying her closely. She smiled with delight, knowing them finally safe and together for good. A knock at the door brought them both fully awake.

"Come in," Crystal called.

Frinz burst through the door, eager to embrace the two she loved so dearly.

"Oh, to see you safe brings me joy! The war is over. Sörnam is vanquished, and the curse has been lifted! Peace is restored once more, thanks to you both!"

They laughed and cried together, hugging each other tightly.

Crystal, overcome, spoke quietly.

"We must remember all who fought to win this battle—those who are here to celebrate as well as those who were lost in the fight."

216

Brant squeezed her hand tightly and said, "We will! We must thank them, every last one of them!"

The three heroes readied themselves and went into the streets, eager to join with the people in celebration. They found the streets crowded with people celebrating and awaiting their arrival. Frinz escorted Crystal and Brant through the throngs of people. They stopped often to shake the hands of grateful men and women.

The people were eager to see the Children of the Prophecy and thank them for the gifts that had been bestowed by the Stone of Power. Already, those gifts were being put to use restoring the crops and erasing the ravages of war from the land. They found Lilly and Basem among the celebrating citizens and ran to embrace their friend tightly.

"Your love, kindness, and power know no bounds," Lilly said, holding them close.

"We thank you as well, Lilly, for all you have done," Brant said warmly.

Basem clapped him on the back and said, "You not only helped to end Sürnam's cursed reign, but you have spread the Stone of Power's magic so that all might share in it."

He snapped his fingers, and a plant sprung from the ground, flourishing instantly into a tree which bore fruit.

"Astounding!" Crystal said, her eyes sparkling with wonder.

Basem continued, "There is much to be done, and you have given us the means to begin repairing centuries of destruction. We thank you."

Crystal and Brant smiled in deference to the thanks and praise they received.

Crystal turned to Lilly and said, "We have all played our parts. Lilly, it was you who ended Sürnam and freed the world from his evil. Tell me, did the Stone of Power grant you special gifts as well?"

Lilly's reply held no regret. "Alas, no, but I believe my gift was the power to help end this war once and for all. The power was hidden deep within, and with it, Sörnam was destroyed. With that, and my true love beside me, I can ask for no greater gift."

Basem held Lilly's hand tight in his and beamed with pride.

Brant and Crystal spent their day greeting the people and enjoying the celebration of victory. They honored those lives lost with tributes and songs. As evening grew near, Frinz beckoned them to the council meeting where the leaders would discuss Garzula and its fate.

Crystal and Brant were pleased with the council's decision to tear down all remnants of Sörnam's reign and rebuild the lands for the growing population. Where once had been terror and hate, now would the people live and prosper. A memorial would stand where the castle had loomed, a beautiful tribute to those who perished.

When the council adjourned, Zabrina joined their group, bringing with her friends—new and old. Angerwin and Drinin arrived and introduced Crystal and Brant to Hallin. Gone was the curse, and Hallin's eyes glowed amber in the twilight. He nestled close to his new companions, grateful beyond words.

"Crystal, Brant," said a voice from behind them.

Brant and Crystal turned to see Bahra bowing before them. Her people kneeled behind her, showing the respect due their heroes.

"You have succeeded beyond our wildest imaginings, Children of the Prophecy," Bahra began, tears glistening behind her yellow eyes.

"We thank you for vanquishing evil from this land. We return to our homes to begin anew, welcoming all into our woods that we may share the land. All is as it should be."

Crystal gave a tearful smile. "That's a wonderful thing to hear."

Angerwin spoke next.

"I will travel with Hallin and Drinin to the distant lands in hopes that we may seek out dragons that have long fled Thurnangl. Perhaps our story will compel them to return to their homeland."

"And we," said Frinz, patting Crystal on the head, "are going to go home. Mardra and Liane eagerly await news of all that has transpired."

"Yes! Let's go home," Crystal and Brant said.

They flew to the cottage in the woods as the sun set behind them. Brant and Crystal noticed a change in the land. Color and life abounded. The grass was green and lush, and everywhere, flowers were blooming. The land and its people were truly thriving.

The cottage was a welcome sight, and Mardra was at their side before Zabrina had fully landed. The travelers jumped from the dragon's back and into the arms of their waiting companions who could do no more than cry and laugh. Whiticker jumped from Liane's arms into Crystal's, overjoyed at her return.

The day was spent in preparation for the celebratory feast. As they made ready for their guests, they talked of all that had happened. Liane had been granted the power to read a book just by touching it, and Mardra could communicate with the unseen souls of those who had gone before. She spoke often to the specter of her husband, whose presence brought her new peace and comfort.

Mardra spoke quietly to her daughter of the father and husband they had lost.

"Your father is very proud of you, his beautiful daughter, and all you have accomplished."

Frinz eyes welled with tears, and she whispered, "Tell my Father thank you and that I love him beyond words."

Mardra smiled and kissed Frinz gently. "He hears you, my child. He loves you deeply."

Frinz wrapped her arms around her mother's neck, unable to speak further.

They talked of their adventures and the gifts the Stone of Power had granted to all in Thurnangl, but none could account for Frinz as she had no new power to speak of.

"I think," said Frinz, a secret smile on her face, "that my gift was granted long before the rest. I was given the power to seek out the Children of the Prophecy and help you see your destiny through. What greater gift could there be?"

They smiled at her revelation, for only the truest of hearts could find contentment in the joy of others.

Preparations continued as evening approached. Frinz left them to answer a knock at the door and returned, arm in arm with Arron. They moved immediately to stand before Mardra, and Arron took the woman's hand.

"Dearest Mardra, I have come to ask for your blessing of our marriage."

A collective gasp met his words, and Mardra beamed through tears.

"My son, I wish you all the blessings in the world!"

Her words were accompanied by the tears and laughter of loved ones celebrating their good fortune and the future to come.

Brant and Crystal excused themselves shortly after dinner and retired to their room. Crystal flopped onto her bed, and Whiticker nestled close.

"So what are we going to do now?" Brant asked.

"Well," Crystal said, lifting her head from her pillow, "we can't stay here forever. We both know that."

"Are you going to leave, Crystal?" Whiticker asked in a sad voice.

Brant sat next to Crystal's bed. "We don't want to leave this place, but we want to go home too. We haven't seen our parents in months, and we miss them a lot."

"So what are you going to do?" Whiticker asked.

Crystal and Brant looked at each other and smiled. They knew exactly what they would do.

The next morning, Crystal and Brant made their way to the kitchen wearing their clothes from home. Though worn, they would suffice for the journey back. Conversation stopped as their friends studied them closely.

Frinz mustered a smile. "Are ready to return home so soon?"

Crystal and Brant nodded.

Frinz continued, knowing this day would come, "You must do what your hearts tell you is right. Long have you been absent from your families. We cannot keep you forever."

"But we won't stay away forever either," Brant said.

Everyone's eyes widened in surprise.

"Thurnangl is as much a part of us now as we are of it. We can't just leave and never come back. We want to be here, every weekend if you'll have us. We'll be in our world for school and here to take part in Thurnangl's restoration."

Crystal giggled at the shocked looks around her.

"We'll tell our parents everything. They have a right to know what we've been through. We will no longer stop time to visit. Instead, we'll grow, sharing the experiences of both worlds."

Liane sighed happily. "You are right, my children. The Stone of Power, as intertwined as you are, will bring you to Thurnangl as you wish. Your tale must be told, and though it be hard, your parents will understand. You will show them the truth of your words."

Crystal touched the scars still on her face, and Brant squeezed her hand. Crystal could not help but beam.

They said their goodbyes, knowing them to be temporary. Crystal and Brant, accompanied by Whiticker, Zabrina and Frinz, made their way to the Stone of Power. Flying swiftly, they reached their destination by sundown and set down next to a magnificent tree that had sprung magically on the hilltop. Its boughs were vast and it reached toward the heavens as though it had stood thousands of years.

"Where did it come from?" Crystal asked, as Whiticker jumped onto her shoulder.

Zabrina answered, her voice solemn with respect, "A tree symbolizes the four great elements. It gathers sustenance from the sun, the greatest fire of all. It requires water to live and thrive. Its roots are planted firmly in the earth, and it cleans the air so that we may breathe."

"It is magnificent," Whiticker whispered in awe.

Frinz was much affected by the sight of Crystal and Brant standing together where their journey had begun. Here too would it end.

Crystal smiled. Recognizing the sadness in Frinz's eyes, she took her friend's hands.

"Our journey will never truly end, dear Frinz. Every time we step onto this land, it begins anew. We will carry our story always, letting it shape and change us, and sharing it with others who will carry on our legacy."

Trying her very best to hold back the tears, Frinz kissed each of them on the forehead.

"I will see you soon, yes?"

"Yes," they said together.

Brant and Crystal each placed a hand on the tree, and a light surrounded them. They looked back and caught a last glimpse of the land they had grown to love and the friends who would remain in their hearts forever.

Hand in hand they went forth, ready for the next adventure.

CHAPTER 31
FIFTEEN YEARS LATER

"Mommy! Mommy!" squealed the little girl, running down the hall and launching herself at her mother.

"Why, whatever is the matter, Ellie?" Crystal asked her tiny daughter, the hint of a smile on her lips.

"Jacob pushed me, Mommy!" Eleanor wailed, burying her face in Crystal's skirt.

Crystal looked into the face of her five-year-old and said with feigned sincerity, "Well then, we must ask him to apologize."

Brant, standing nearby, laughed at his wife before turning to their son.

"Well, young man?"

At seven, Jacob was the eldest child and a rather solemn boy. His father's green eyes stared out of a face that marked him clearly as Crystal's son. Where Eleanor bore the darker hair and complexion of her father, Jacob favored his mother completely. They were perfect representations of the love their parents shared. At the young boy's feet, Whiticker snickered, and Jacob looked up to see his parents doing the same.

"Jacob," Brant warned, "please apologize to your sister."

"Sorry, Ellie," Jacob said.

"It's ok, big brother, I'm not hurt," Ellie giggled.

Mardra walked into the hall, welcoming them with a laugh, "My, my! Such a fuss can only mean that visitors have arrived!"

"Grandma Mardra!" the children exclaimed, running into the elderly woman's embrace. Their parents looked on, Brant holding Crystal close, as Whiticker trotted after his young charges.

Mardra beckoned them toward the kitchen where the rest of the party had already assembled. Lilly and Basem welcomed them with a smile. Their teenage son, Sidwell—the spitting image of his handsome father—lifted Ellie into his arms and spun her around as they laughed.

Frinz and Arron could only wave as the children rushed to greet each other. Their son, Galen, was growing into a fine young man of thirteen, as handsome as his father and grandfather. Roselyn had recently turned nine, and she was as lovely as her mother, with fiery hair and violet eyes that would soon mark her as a beauty.

The children ran about, playing games and screaming with Whiticker at their side. Ellie ran to Zabrina and clung to her neck. Zabrina raised her head, and the little girl squealed as her feet were lifted from the ground.

"Thank you so much for hosting all of us, Mardra," Brant said.

"Oh, it is no trouble, my dear. It is worth it to hear them call me 'Grandma Mardra.'" Mardra paused, looking past Brant to an empty corner of the room. She smiled tenderly as she continued, "Grandpa Malchior is grateful as well."

Crystal moved to where Frinz and Lilly stood. The three women embraced as they watched the children at play.

"Did you ever once think that we would end up like this?" Crystal asked.

Love and pure joy welled in her heart as she watched the young ones

"Yes," said Frinz, "the day you two came back for the first time with your parents."

They laughed together as their hearts swelled with pride. Sidwell played with the young Ellie as Galen and Jacob ran about with Roselyn. Their children were lovely, brave creatures, made better by the shared past of their parents. Brant wrapped his arms around his wife's shoulders and kissed her cheek gently.

"We're watching their adventures unfold now," he said with a smile.

Crystal beamed, imaging what was to come for their young ones.

Arron chuckled, embracing Frinz.

"This would be a much bigger party if we were to invite Drinin and Angerwin. Their daughter, Cornelia, is growing by leaps and bounds."

"Dragons do grow faster than children," Basem said laughingly.

"But there are so many young dragons now that there is always fun to be had with our children and their children," said Lilly.

Brant spoke proudly, his eyes never leaving the joyous site before him, "Our children will grow and play together, keeping our story alive."

Frinz smiled.

"In both your world and ours, the story will be told forever."

The End

ACKNOWLEDGEMENTS

For my mother, for putting up with me and being the light on my darkest of days. Your words will always guide me.

For my father, who taught me what true inner strength is. You will find the kindness and strength of these male heroes comes from you.

For my sister, whose unconditional love is laden in these pages. You showed me what true love is.

For my brother, for always motivating and inspiring me. I adore you to the ends of the earth.

For my husband, for cheering me on even when I wanted to give in. For drying my tears of frustration, and giving me strength. You are my hero, always.

For my children, for changing my life in a way I never thought possible. Your very existence gave me a reason to achieve my dreams. Never let anything in life stand in the way of your dreams.

For my friends, new and old, for having my back, holding my hand, and never letting me fall. Many of you will find yourselves within these pages if you look hard enough.

To Lilian Diep, who was essential to bringing the original Thurnangl story to publication. Your guidance and support gave Thurnangl the legs upon which it now stands.

To K.P. Expressions Photography for my beautiful author photo.

To Chris Simpson, illustrator extraordinaire, who perfectly captured the heart of this magical land in your amazing artwork.

To Demond and Elizabeth of A Book Nerd Company, thank you for the incredible opportunity you have given me. Thank you for your tireless work, your dedication, and your incredible friendship. Thurnangl would not be without you.

And to you, the reader, for being here for the journey to the very end, thank you.

ABOUT THE AUTHOR

Kimberly Byrd is a wife and mother who takes delight in sharing stories like Thurnangl with the world. Kimberly's artistic expression extends far beyond her writing and finds an outlet in her professional photography business.

Born in Texas to a military family, Mrs. Byrd credits the love and support of her family as the inspiration behind her first published work, "Thurnangl." She shares her time between writing, running her professional photography business, and raising her young children.

Her husband's military career has allowed Kimberly to experience much of the United States and inspired the adventures found in her works. With her eye for beauty and heart for the written word, Mrs. Byrd's dearest wish is that others might take joy in her work and share in the adventures which play out in the pages of her stories.

CPSIA information can be obtained
at www.ICGtesting.com
Printed in the USA
BVHW031912150319
542803BV00001B/2/P